Acclaim for
Confessions of a Male Nurse

"This sometimes-shocking account of the experience of a gay male nurse will provoke many emotions among readers. We need to welcome this kind of discussion of the coming-of-age of a professional. Ferri's moving—and often humorous—story of this journey as a nurse is long overdue."

—Suzanne Gordon, Author,
Nursing Against the Odds:
How Health Care Cost-Cutting,
Media Stereotypes, and Medical Hubris
Undermine Nurses and Patient Care

"*Confessions of a Male Nurse* is a very funny book; a current of jest runs through it as medical professionals perform both misdeed and, sometimes, the miraculous. Ferri's writing is smooth, breezy, punctuated with the quick curses of startled, stymied people laboring as well as they can. But in truth, it is a serious book, if rarely somber, and speaks of ill training, guesswork, and mismanagement, and the resultant tragedies that should have been abridged but, in the harried atmosphere of the hospital, were not.

Ferri's purpose is not to moralize. The book is the narrative of a young gay man who becomes a nurse and sees many a bumble, many a misfire, as well as stamina and courage. It is, finally, the fact of disease and mortality that is the opposition, not human imperfection. Having been so well entertained and shed much laughter, we see this with sudden, pulse-quickening clarity. This is a brave book."

—Mary Oliver, Author,
Pulitzer Prize-winning
American Primitive

"A chronicle of the adventures of Steele, a gay man who defies the odds to become a first-rate nurse and unexpectedly finds true love, Richard Ferri's *Confessions of a Male Nurse* is by turns an uproarious, tender, and deadly serious journey through the medical profession, the wild NYC social scene of the late 70s and early 80s, and the bumpy terrain of the human heart.

This riotous and absorbing tale puts truth behind every outrage, farce in every observation, and pulls no punches along the way. In quick succession you'll laugh, you'll be scandalized, you'll cry, and then you'll laugh through your tears. Richard Ferri's perfect pitch for the wicked wisecrack and his deft way of mixing the sublime with the ridiculous make him a rare writer and his book a delightful read. His characters are too alive to let go at the end. If we're lucky, he won't let the saga end here."

—Luciano Guerriero, Author,
The Spin, Brooklyn Noir,
and *Chicago Noir*

Confessions
of a Male Nurse

HARRINGTON PARK PRESS®
Southern Tier Editions™
Gay Men's Fiction

The Man Pilot by James W. Ridout IV

Shadows of the Night: Queer Tales of the Uncanny and Unusual edited by Greg Herren

Van Allen's Ecstasy by Jim Tushinski

Beyond the Wind by Rob N. Hood

The Handsomest Man in the World by David Leddick

The Song of a Manchild by Durrell Owens

The Ice Sculptures: A Novel of Hollywood by Michael D. Craig

Between the Palms: A Collection of Gay Travel Erotica edited by Michael T. Luongo

Aura by Gary Glickman

Love Under Foot: An Erotic Celebration of Feet edited by Greg Wharton and M. Christian

The Tenth Man by E. William Podojil

Upon a Midnight Clear: Queer Christmas Tales edited by Greg Herren

Dryland's End by Felice Picano

Whose Eye Is on Which Sparrow? by Robert Taylor

Deep Water: A Sailor's Passage by E. M. Kahn

The Boys in the Brownstone by Kevin Scott

The Best of Both Worlds: Bisexual Erotica edited by Sage Vivant and M. Christian

Tales from the Levee by Martha Miller

Some Dance to Remember: A Memoir-Novel of San Francisco 1970-1982 by Jack Fritscher

Confessions of a Male Nurse by Richard S. Ferri

The Millionaire of Love by David Leddick

Transgender Erotica: Trans Figures edited by M. Christian

Skip Macalester by J. E. Robinson

Chemistry by Lewis DeSimone

Friends, Lovers, and Roses by Vernon Clay

Beyond Machu by William Maltese

Virgina Bedfellows by Gavin Morris

Independent Queer Cinema: Reviews and Interviews by Gary M. Kramer

Seventy Times Seven by Salvatore Sapienza

Going Down in La-La Land by Andy Zeffer

Planting Eli by Jeff Black

Confessions
of a Male Nurse

Richard S. Ferri

Southern Tier Editions™
Harrington Park Press®
An Imprint of The Haworth Press, Inc.
New York • London • Oxford

Published by

Southern Tier Editions™, Harrington Park Press®, an imprint of The Haworth Press, Inc., 10 Alice Street, Binghamton, NY 13904-1580.

PUBLISHER'S NOTE
This is a work of fiction. Names, characters, places, and incidents either are the products of the author's imagination or are used fictitiously, and any resemblance to actual persons, living or dead, business establishments, events, or locales is entirely coincidental.

ISBN: 978-0-7394-6422-9

For John E White
You are my home.

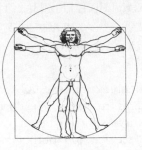

PART ONE

"It's a boy! Mr. Steele," the nurse says with great relief. "A fine, healthy baby boy, and your wife . . ."

"I don't want a goddamn boy. Son of bitch! Can't she do anything right?" My father yells.

The nurse walks over to my father and slaps his face.

"Just two hours ago I had to walk in here and tell another father that his baby was dead," she hisses. "Get the fuck out of my hospital you asshole!"

My father leaves.

I am three years old and have not had a bowel movement without screaming for several months. I am sick. I am in a hospital. My mother has just left to go home. I stand up in the corner of my crib and cry at the top of my lungs: "Nurse! Nurse! Nurse!" Within an instant some total stranger in a white uniform and a silly looking hat comes into my room and holds me. I feel safe. I will spend the good part of the night going from one nurse to another, my feet never touching the ground.

I am ten years old and clutching my mother's hand in an emergency room. My mother is barely breathing. Our eyes are glued to a door. A grim-faced physician comes out followed by a nurse.

"I am sorry Mrs. Steele but we weren't able to save your husband." The doctor touches my mother's shoulders then walks away.

My mother holds me as tightly as I hold her. The nurse bends down and whispers to me. "Even big boys like you get to cry when their daddy dies." I cry.

My back has a severe double curvature. At age thirteen I am nearly totally bent over. My mother is frustrated. The doctor that has been treating me keeps saying that the curve is getting better. Of course it's not. Any fool, except the fool doctor, can see that. My mother does not know what to do. I am a teenager who is embarrassed by my very physical being. My mother gets a call from a mother of a classmate of mine. She has never met my mother, but has seen me numerous times on the playground. She knows what is wrong with me. Her daughter has it too. She gives my mother the name of her daughter's surgeon. Finally, I will be treated.

The treatment for my back requires nearly a year of hospitalization on total bed rest. I have the two major surgeries and nearly become despondent during the ordeal. No one knows what is wrong with me. The physicians, social workers, and even the pink ladies stand over my bed and shake their heads in wonder.

"What could be wrong? He is so young, so much to look forward to."

What is wrong is that I am depressed. My father is dead and my mother is working two jobs. I have not walked in about eight months and have had two very painful operations. The pain from the major surgery is incredible, but no one thinks that a teenager needs pain medicine. I suffer. My skin erupts into the single most horrendous case of acne in the history of civilization. I have no privacy. I think I am a thirteen-year-old about to lose his mind.

Miss Collins, the nurse who has been taking care of me all these months comes into my room on her day off and says, "It's tough, isn't it? Let's talk." We talk.

Father Gerald Francis is standing in front of the room. He is very strict, but he is a favorite of all the boys at Holy Name Boy's Preparatory School. He is terrific to have in class if you can get him after lunch and his gin. His afternoon classes are wild. He gives you the answers to his tests and talks about sex. However, while sober he is just to the right of Attila the Hun. Today we have him in the morning. Today is a Saturday, but we are all at school in our mandatory jackets and ties. We are about to take a college entrance exam, and we had better not screw it up Father Gerald Francis yells. If we screw up something as simple as a test how in the hell are we ever going to get to Vietnam and kill for Jesus. Good question, but many of us do not plan to go to Vietnam and kill for anybody. Father says we should.

He hands out the sealed test booklets and answer sheets. No one is breathing. This is the moment of truth. Will we be able to get into a college, any college, and stay out of the army?

Father Gerald Francis stands before us and sways a little to the left. His voice is loud and somewhat out of control. I think he needs a drink. A little gin right now wouldn't hurt. I realize that I am scared. I will never be able to get into college. I am not smart. I wonder how hot it gets in Vietnam.

"You boys will follow my directions," he announces. "You will only do what I tell you to after I tell you to do it." Father then goes on to explain the great blacken-the-dot ritual of the answer sheet. We have all heard it before hundreds of times. We pretend to listen. I fantasize about the boy sitting next to me. Damn, even his head is a huge muscle.

"Now down here in the lower left-hand corner there is a box labeled nursing scholarships. If any of you gentleman, or should I say *ladies,* would like to be eligible for a New York State nursing scholarship blacken in that space." He stares out to see if anyone would dare blacken that box.

The entire class laughingly snorts in reply, myself included. Mark Stedman, the boy sitting alphabetically in front of me, turns and says, "Only a real homo would go to nursing school."

"Yea," I say.

Eventually I go to nursing school and come out as a gay man. So you see, some things do work out.

I am accepted into only one college. I have been put on the waiting list at the others. The college that is willing to take me is a dump, and I last one semester. Off to the world of work and I end up being a minimum-wage file clerk for Florida land developers that do not sell to blacks. I do not see any great future in this position.

One day during my fifteen-minute coffee break I decide that I will become a laboratory technician. I decide that what I really want to do with my life is walk around a hospital in a smart lab coat and stick needles in people. What could be more satisfying?

I call the local hospital and ask to speak to someone about how to become a laboratory technician. The voice on the other end of the phone says she doesn't know who could give me that information, but maybe someone in the school of nursing could help out. Swell.

No one at the nursing school knows about how to become a laboratory technician. However, would I like an application to their school? They have a program starting in the fall. Sure, I say. Three months later I am off to nursing school. I make the most important decision of my life on the advice a switchboard operator that I will never meet. Oh well.

I simply fall into the profession of nursing. In high school my career guidance test said I should become either a priest or a podiatrist. I think those two vocations combined pretty much sum up what it takes to become a nurse. Blood and compassion.

Nursing school is a rehearsal for hell. I go through the good old-fashioned diploma program where you get to spend three years of your life working and studying like a dog for a piece of paper that isn't a college degree. We will have three weeks off in the summer and two at Christmas. We also get free on-campus housing, which translates into slave quarters. All the students are required to live on campus, except the married ones, so that they can devote their full energies to studying. Bullshit. We all have to live at the hospital because we are cheap free labor. Anytime there is a big disaster, or a snowstorm, or an outbreak of the flu the students have to go in and work the night shift. It's good experience, they say. You would never get this in one of those fancy college programs.

I also wouldn't get addicted to caffeine and liquor, I say. *Well, if you feel that way, Mr. Steele, you can just pack up your bags and go back to that wonderful career you had going.* I try to look remorseful. I need to stay in nursing school. I have no other place to go. I am broke. I am certainly not scholarship material. So I act contrite and do floor duty anytime the phone rings.

Do not get any benevolent thoughts about my attitude—there isn't much choice. During the winter the students are hit hard. We are pulling an average of two nights a week floor duty and there is never any acceptable excuse to miss class. I work from eleven at night to seven in the morning and class starts at eight. Lunchtime I shower and nap. By the end of the first year of nursing school I am existing on peanut butter stolen from the pediatric floor, vodka, and gallons of coffee. This, of course, is topped off with as many cigarettes as I can smoke. We have a theory why nearly everyone in our class smokes: it is the only excuse you can give for sitting down. *Hey Mrs. Greene, I am going to catch a smoke, okay? Sure, go ahead. Hey Mrs. Greene, I am going to sit down for five minutes because my feet are killing me, okay? Sure, sit down and take care of those feet while the patients lie around in their own shit!* Student nurses smoke to absolve ourselves from the guilt of being human.

During my first summer off from school I stay in my dorm room for the first few days and sleep. We get to keep our rooms because we only have the three weeks off. I finally wake up and realize that my vacation is almost over. I have about seventy bucks to my name. Not bad really. I was able to save that much from the twenty-five-dollar weekly stipend they give us. Well, they don't actually give it to us—they bestow it. Like it was some big deal. I mean they get their money's worth.

I stand naked and alone in my room. I look in the mirror. I have lost twenty pounds. I am now 5' 7" with the resounding weight of 147 pounds. I look at my reflection and I realize that this is the first time since I started nursing school that I have really looked at a human body without tubes. I turn around. Not bad really. Nice legs. Nice firm butt. No catheters or respirator. Count your lucky stars.

I decide that I need to relax. Translation: I need to get laid. Sort of God's little joke on gay men, putting us with all these young and willing females and no desire on our part. Right now, all I want is a little homosexual lust.

I call my friend Carmella and tell her I want to go to the Glory Hole, the only gay bar I know, and she says sure. She'll pick me up around ten. Swell.

The Glory Hole is one of the sleaziest places that I know. It is located in the bowels of Yonkers, like there is any other section, right? The bar is the only building on a deserted block that isn't boarded up and smelling of urine. There are no signs. No lights. No indication that there is anything there at all except block after block of parked cars. I figure this is the only gay bar in the entire state of New York and people must come from all over. God, I make a box of hammers look smart.

Carmella shows up at 9:45 p.m. She has this annoying habit of being early. There is a knock on my door. I yell for her to come in. She is dressed in her white nurse's uniform. I glare at her.

"Okay, so kill me already. I have to go in at midnight. Look they called. Everyone is out sick with some fucking bug or something." She fishes for a cigarette from her purse. I just continue to stare at her. I am pissed. "What in the fuck was I suppose to do? Let all the patients die?"

"They won't die. I know that I am just a first-year, no make that a second-year nursing student and you are already a big time LPN, but they will get along just fine without you for one night. Besides, I was hoping to pick somebody up at the Glory Hole tonight, and you know that I always do better when you're there."

Carmella sucks on her cigarette and attempts Bette Davis.

"Just what I always wanted to be . . . the first nurse fag hag!"

"Sweetheart, you would hardly be the first. And by the way, that was a wonderful Ralph Bellamy you just did."

"For your information Mr. Smart-ass-I-am-going-to-be-an-RN-and-you-are-not, that was Florence Nightingales' younger half sister, Golda."

"Golda Nightingale?"

"An unrecognized patron of our founding mother."

"Oh yea? What did she do?"

"She nagged. Flo never would have left that upper-crust life if Golda didn't kvetch until she dropped."

"You should teach nursing history."

"Honey, I plan to be nursing history."

We laugh and off we go into the hot summer night. One angel of mercy, and one semiliterate hopeful.

The men at the Glory Hole are all alike. I am beginning to wonder if there are a set of secret rules that must be followed in order to be gay.

> Rule number one: Always look bored but horny.
> Rule number two: Always know the complete lyrics to the latest songs.
> Rule number three: Never commit.
> Rule number four: Never make fun of Judy Garland.
> Rule number five: Be very serious about your career as an assistant buyer of men's clothing for Macy's.

I decide that I do not like any rules I must live by. There are just too many stereotypes. I tell this to Carmella. She reminds me that I am studying to become a nurse. So? I say. So, she says back, was the beautician course filled?

I admit it that I am just another homosexual stereotype. A gay male nurse. Who would have guessed?

Carmella and I drink and smoke and talk shop. It is 11:30 p.m. Carmella orders another round. A blackberry brandy for herself, and a Southern

Comfort on the rocks for me. We drink down our respective syrups. I am beginning to feel hopeful. I begin to beg Carmella to call in sick. Let the bitch on the evening shift stay over for once.

Carmella calls the hospital and tells them she is suddenly ill. Having terrible cramps. The worst period of all time.

We stay until 4:00 a.m. I go home with some guy who looked cute through booze and dim lighting. In the morning I am horrified. I tell myself the standard lie. Never again.

I spend the entire summer vacation in various states of consciousness at the Glory Hole. I find no love of my life, but who says I'm looking?

School begins again and we are all sitting in the auditorium. Mrs. Finch, the director of the school, is standing before us. I am staring at her tits. I try to figure out how she gets them so pointy. They look like two teepees trying to pop out of her uniform. She gives the same speech as she gave last year. Probably the same speech she gives every year. She tells us, with a special emphasis for the incoming class, that nearly twenty-five percent of us sitting in the room will never graduate. We will never be nurses. Take a good look around because the person sitting next to you may not be here next week. The freshman class is frozen into silence. The junior and seniors just groan. We know that it is true, but who the hell wants to hear it?

Next, Mrs. Finch commands, there are no excuses for being sick. If we plan to be sick maybe we should become patients instead of nurses. If for some reason we are truly ill we must never miss more than three days of class. Missing that much time simply cannot be made up and we will be dropped from the program. Finally, if we should ever develop such a severe case of sunburn that we cannot come to class we are automatically dismissed. Sunburn is a self-inflicted injury.

I smile. I remember last year when some of the girls fell asleep in the sun and had to show up the next day for operating-room orientation. The only part of them that showed was their bulging eyes. The entire rest of their bodies were covered in heavy green scrubs and sterile gowns that are washed in a lye-based detergent.

I look around the room. From my calculations there are about eight people missing from my class. Dropouts, I figure. Later in the dorm we will talk about them like the subhuman losers that they really are. There is no greater calling than this, and if you can't meet it, well—fuck off. Not exactly a saintly attitude, but as the saying goes, fuck off.

What I do see is the other fool male student. Mike Wolfe is an asshole. He is about my age, good looking, and constantly on the edge. He tries to keep his heterosexuality in a highly visible position. He appears to enjoy spitting and picking his nose. His other favorite pursuits are to be as disheveled as possible within our strict dress code. He also enjoys hanging out with the orderlies and talking about snatch.

This asshole and I have become inevitable partners for any laboratory sessions. Mrs. Finch says she likes to keep her boys together. Well, who doesn't? Everyone assumes that we will become fast and fabulous friends. In the beginning I did try. I will even say that Mike tried, somewhat. But if the truth be known we simply did not hit it off because he is an idiot and I'm not.

Mike notices me looking at him and shifts uncomfortably in his seat. I smile as big a smile as I can. I love to make him nervous. You see, Mike has this stupid heterosexual framework from which he operates. He assumes that everything anybody does is related to sex. He has confused his brain with his penis. Both of which are probably the same size, and that is not saying much for either of them. Since I am gay he automatically knows that my whole existence is predicated on getting into his straight pants. Mike needs to put his gonads in perspective.

The second year of nursing school will be different than the first we are told. Damn well better be, I think. I certainly don't want to put up with that shit again. There will be no more uniform inspections for the upper classes. No more surprise knocks on my dorm door at 5 a.m. wanting to check the crease in my pants or the white of my shoes. For this I am grateful.

The goal of our first year was to get all of the basic science courses like anatomy and chemistry behind us. We were introduced to the clinical setting where we functioned with the skill and expertise of a bad nurse's aide. Now, in our second year, we will begin our specialty rotations. Medical-surgical nursing. Pediatrics. Obstetrics. Operating room. Intensive care. Psychiatry.

I find out that I am going to do my psych rotation first. Three months in the loony bin. I am nervous about being around the crazies. I identify with them too strongly. The only good thing is that Mike and I are finally separated. He is off to deliver substandard care to some poor slob of a kid on the pediatrics ward.

Mrs. Zvibleman, affectionately known as Mrs. Z, is the instructor for the psych course. Unfortunately, Mrs. Z suffers from the same sad fate of all psych nurses—she is crazier than any of her patients. Mrs. Z is somewhat doughy in appearance with overworked hair that lost its original hue years ago. A mad dash of red lipstick always accents her teeth as well as her lips.

"Class, welcome to the world of psychiatric nursing," she says on our first class day. "No other nursing specialty is as rewarding as this. Dealing with those who cannot cope is truly the nurse's job."

No one wears white uniforms in psych. I guess they give the patients the willies. Mrs. Z wears the same thing everyday. Black stretch pants and sweaters with hundreds of little synthetic pills. She looks very much like a mad French woman recovering from a nervous breakdown.

"There are a few rules we need to establish before we begin our journey into the world of the mind." She begins to walk around the room touching each of us as she passes. "Never be afraid to show that you care. Let the patient know that you accept him as he is. That is the first and great rule. We, as nurses, accept people for what they are. We do not judge. We evaluate. We do not insist on behavior to be a certain way. We accept."

Mrs. Z stands in the back of the room and whispers, "Now class, please close your eyes and put your heads down on your desk. Come now, don't be shy. You must learn to trust." She waits until all of our heads are down and our eyes are closed. Her voice is soft and very low. I almost fall asleep.

"There is something very important that you must understand about working in psych," she soothes. "A very, very important thing. Another rule really. Something so important that if you ever forget it even just once I will fuck you over in this program for good. I will cut your nuts off, so to speak. Now, what could be so important to get Mrs. Z so miffed?" She pauses then yells. "Loonies! Crazies! Nut jobs! If I ever hear, or think I hear any of you, use those or other terms to describe a patient on the psychiatric unit I will have your ass." Another pause. I do not think anyone in the room is breathing. "Now before we lift our heads let anyone who didn't quite understand me raise their hand." She waits for some fool to be her first victim. No one moves.

"Good," she beams. "Now, lets all sit up and rub our little eyes so we can see the world clearly." Nearly skipping to the front of the room she is positively gushing with her arms flapping about. "Welcome, welcome my little ones. You are going to positively love it! I'm so excited for you. Let's all meet in the cafeteria tomorrow morning at six and I will tell you all about the adventures that await you on Kleinburg Five!"

What awaits us on Kleinburg Five is a locked floor of twenty-five adult loonies who sit around all day playing hearts, smoking cigarettes, drinking water, and lining up for pills.

The Archangel Gabriel also awaits me in the form of Sally Schumacher, a forty-year-old mother of twelve illegitimate children from twelve different fathers. She is standing on top of a card table, her arms stretched out like wings. Three other women are playing cards around her feet.

"I am the blessed Archangel Gabriel bringing you glad tidings! I have been sent because I am pure. I am chaste."

"Honey, the only thing you are is an old whore," one of the card-playing women hacks between drags of her cigarette.

"I am not!"

"Honey, you've had so many weenies in you even Oscar Mayer has a picture of you in his office."

The card-playing women laugh through thick clouds of cigarette smoke.

"Gabby darling, why don't you just let us Mellaril mamas play cards. Why don't you go talk to them nice new student nurses. I am sure that they would love to hear about your virginity." Looking directly at me the oldest-looking card player says, "Go talk to that nice young homo over there. My my ladies," she says back to her cronies, "isn't he just the handsomest thing. Sure wouldn't mind having a piece of him."

Getting up from the table she walks directly to me. I do not move. I am being therapeutic. I will not allow her to develop this interaction into a personal confrontation. I clearly do not have the slightest notion of what I am doing.

"How big?"

I just look at her.

"How big is your dick, baby?" she screams as she grabs for my crotch and twists it with the strength of mother trying to open a jar of jelly.

My immediate response is simple. I faint dead away and drop to the floor as I scream and revert to a fetal position. I can hear people asking her to explain her behavior. A staff nurse suggests to her that her actions were inappropriate and that maybe a few hours in seclusion would be good for her. A psychiatrist steps over me to tell her that he did not like her behavior. I am laying on the floor plotting on how to kill the bitch.

Mrs. Z finally comes over and bends down to me. "Did she hurt you Richard?"

I nod assent. Nurses are tough. We don't normally display such outbursts of emotion.

"Here, let Mrs. Z help you up." I am trying to remember to look up the disorder that is associated with referring to yourself in the third person.

Mrs. Z helps me to the nurse's lounge as I do my best imitation of Groucho. She tells me to lay on the couch that is half covered with old journals and used coffee cups. She takes my pulse.

"A little fast," she says. "I suppose that is to be expected."

"Now, let Mrs. Z see."

I stare at her.

"Oh, don't be such a silly," she says as she reaches for my zipper. "Remember, Mrs. Z is a nurse. We must check to be sure that no real damage has been done." With the acquired skill of a streetwalker she pulls down my pants. I never wear underwear and my dick pops out.

"Oh my," she says. "It's not swollen?"

I look down. It's not swollen.

"Oh my, Oh my, Oh my!"

The look in Mrs. Z's eyes are giving me the creeps. I am not in the habit of whipping out my dick at school.

I am allowed to rest for fifteen minutes before going back to the unit. As I carefully walk down the hall back toward the nurses' station I see Mrs. Z knock on a door to the seclusion room where my attacker has been taken.

Softly but clearly I hear her say, "He's got eight big ones!" Mrs Z then continues down the hall.

The rest of my psych rotation proves uneventful except for the case of the three-hundred-pound man with bubblegum in his ears. He says he is an atom bomb and the only thing keeping him from exploding is the gum. I find this logical.

The psych nurses put Mr. A-bomb into group therapy. He sits there for hours and never says a word. No matter who yells at him or how loud. He just sits there for weeks. No one appears to know what to do for this guy. Finally, during one of the last staff conferences, a solution is offered by a member of the housekeeping staff.

"Why don't you take the damn gum out of his fool ears," Mrs. Brown says as she mops over our shoes.

Oh.

With great pantomime and spastic charades the gum is removed, and the man explodes. He begins a low but steady moan that grows into a never-ending crescendo. With the agility of a ballet dancer he leaps around the room throwing whatever object he can grab. Within two-and-a-half minutes there is nothing left of the patients' lounge except for twisted metal furniture and broken glass. The staff, students, and patients run to the end of the hall and huddle together. Nuts and bolts together.

"I think he could use some sedation," states a doctor.

"No shit," says Gabriel.

Mr. A-bomb stands at the other end of the hallway. Halfway between him and us is the medication closet.

"Okay Mr. Steele, here are the keys. Just go down the hall and get 100 milligrams of Thorazine IM from the med room."

I slowly turn around to see what idiot has spoken. It is Mrs. Z. She hands me the keys and flashes her lipstick-stained teeth at me.

Mr. A-bomb begins bashing his head against the wall. Without any common sense I take the keys from Mrs. Z and dash down the hall. I figure Mr. A-bomb is too busy abusing his cranium to care about me. I am wrong.

As soon as I get into the medication room he flies into its doorway yelling, "Boom! Boom! Boom!"

I freeze and realize how stupid it is for me to be the one to go after the medication. I don't know how to give an IM injection.

Mr. A-bomb starts pounding his chest with each "Boom!" as he circles the room. I look hopefully out into the hallway for reinforcements. No such luck.

Each "Boom" is becoming louder, and I can see that his eyes have glazed over. Mr. A-bomb is not on this planet. He stops his circling and looks directly at me and begins pounding his chest furiously. "Boom! Boom! Boom! Booooooooooom!"

Out of the corner of my eye I see an open box of tampons sticking out of someone's purse. I grab them.

Mr. A-bomb moves closer to me. I put a tampon in each hand and raise my arms high above my head. As Mr. A-bomb leans into me face I shove the tampons into his ears.

Startled, Mr. A-bomb holds onto the tampons and stops "Booming!"

"New bomb stoppers," I say.

He smiles and sits on the floor in front of me.

I decided there and then never to set foot again into a psych unit unless I am being involuntary committed.

I meet this nice guy at the Glory Hole. His name is Peter. He actually asks me out on a date without sex being a prerequisite. I accept. He is short but good-looking. He lives by himself. He is a waiter. Just before our first date I have picked out the china and silver patterns, and planned the honeymoon. As the doorbell rings I realize I do not even know his last name. What the hell.

Mike and I cross paths during the first of the med-surg rotations that we will have to go through. By the end of our second year he seems a little more relaxed around me. He has even grunted, on occasion, in my direction as a form of a greeting. I continue to flash him a big smile.

One day Mike and I are told that we will be spending the day in the male genitourinary clinic. We are to perform a bladder catherization under the direction of a physician. I ask why a nurse couldn't show us the procedure. I am informed that female nurses do not do such procedures. Like always I am confused. It would be unladylike I am told. So I suppose that wiping someone's ass is the act of princess.

The catheterization procedure involves taking a long sterile latex tube, known as a catheter, and placing it into a man's bladder via his penis. We are told that this procedure simply does not hurt. It is merely uncomfortable. Okay, I can handle this.

Sometimes these catheters are left in and become indwelling. The purpose is for monitoring urinary output or to irrigate an infected bladder. Okay, I can handle this too.

Mike and I are given over to Dr. Reilly, a man who has consciously devoted his life to urine. Dr. Reilly is tall and fat with a constantly sweaty upper lip. He also always wears rubberized boots that go right up to the knee over his trousers. These create a noticeable squishing sound every time he walks.

Dr. Reilly explains the urinary catheterization procedure to us as if he were describing the first time he saw the *Mona Lisa*. I am impressed by his devotion.

In addition to all the necessary steps that are required to perform the catheterization Mike and I learn that potential for infection is great. In fact, indwelling catheters are one of the major causes of hospital-based infections. Dr. Reilly drills us on sterile technique. After about two hours of lecture he decides to show us the procedure.

"Now boys," Dr. Reilly says, "watch me very carefully. I am going to set up my sterile field." With great skill the doctor unwraps sterile towels and equipment and lays them out in the order that he is going to need them. A patient magically appears behind an exam-room curtain like a game-show door prize.

"I am going to place a catheter into Mr. Figura's bladder for the express purpose of dilating his urethra. It appears that Mr. Figura," says Dr. Reilly nodding to the teenager lying on the stretcher in mortal embarrassment, "is having difficulty voiding. It seems every time he attempts to start a stream burning occurs and he cannot continue. Needless to say, this young man is uncomfortable. I will place the catheter in and drain out any residual urine, get a culture, and, hopefully, dilate the urethra thereby solving the problem."

"Mr. Wolfe, would you please get a 22 French Foley catheter from the closet and drop it on the sterile field while Mr. Steele helps the patient off with his pants." It figures.

Mike goes to the closet, finds the requested-sized catheter, and nearly faints dead away. I have masterfully helped the kid off with his chinos and shorts. I look up to find Mike staring at the catheter. It is almost the size of his thumb in diameter. Mr. Figura's penis appears to disappear from view. Smart.

"Now don't worry young man. This really doesn't hurt. You are going to feel some pressure, but no pain," says Dr. Reilly. I smile at the patient like a dolt. I am thinking he should run for his life. I may not be a great man of medical knowledge but I do know sticking a garden-hose-sized tube into this kid's almost nonexistent weenie is going to hurt like hell. I decided to speak.

"Mr. Figura," I begin hesitantly, "Dr. Reilly is going to have to insert that tube into your bladder and you may indeed feel more than uncomfortable. It may hurt, but it will only be . . ."

"Mr. Steele, I will inform my patients whether or not something is going to hurt. I said it isn't, and it won't!" He is almost spitting the words.

"But Doctor it only seems natural . . ."

"Do I need to call Mrs. Finch about this?"

"I think . . ." Mike attempts.

"Not another word out of either of you." Dr. Reilly is beet red.

The patient is trying to pull up his pants and hit the road.

"Lie down and drop your drawers young man," bellows the doctor.

The patient is nearly frozen in his place with a glazed look of terror etched in his face. He does as he is told.

Dr. Reilly grabs the catheter and Mr. Figura's penis. My eyes are about to bug out of my head. The kid is squirming around with fear. Mike is motionless. I decide to sneeze which causes my head to rub up against the catheter.

"You contaminated the goddamn thing, you fool! I know you did it on purpose. I am going to tell Mrs. Finch. I am going to have your ass for this." He throws the catheter down and storms out of the room.

"And you, Mr. Figura, are going to have your penis," I say.

The kid looks up at me gratefully and cups his groin and says a silent prayer.

"Nice going," Mike smiles.

Peter and I have our first date. I feel just like Donna Reed after her first date with George Bailey in *It's a Wonderful Life*. We actually go out to a restaurant and order food and talk. At 2 a.m. he walks me back to my dorm room and kisses me goodnight. He says he'll call me in the morning. I am floating.

Mrs. Finch is sitting behind her desk with her wig leaning slightly southward. Her nurse's cap is big and tall and pulls at her wig. I imagine that she is as bald as a billiard ball underneath that fifty-percent-polyester bouffant. Her lips are pressed tightly together as to prevent any air from escaping. I am sure that Dr. Reilly has called her and I am about to be handed my walking papers. Mrs. Finch motions for me to sit down. I do.

"It appears that you have some explaining to do Mr. Steele."

I just stare back at her.

"Well young man, do you care to explain how a second-year nursing student's judgment supersedes that of well-respected doctor?"

She waits for my response. Her lips are getting tighter and thinner with each passing second.

"Common sense," I say. What the hell is another cup of water when you are drowning?

"I see." Mrs. Finch returns to silence.

"Well now, it appears that you seem to have all the answers but nothing to say. So I am going to let you sit in my office for the afternoon and just think about what you did. I also want a five-hundred-word essay on the importance of a good doctor-nurse relationship on my desk before rounds tomorrow morning."

I can't believe that I am getting off so lightly. I was hoping for just a suspension and praying that I wouldn't be kicked out. I think about this and realize I should clarify this situation.

"Mrs. Finch, excuse me, but is that all? I am not being kicked out or anything?"

She shakes her head and her wig straightens.

"You're very lucky you did the right thing." She leaves me alone in her office.

I take advantage of the time and begin the punishment assignment. I realize that the last time I had a punishment assignment was from Sister Mary Blanche in the seventh grade. Sister was whacking me on the head with her rosary beads for not doing my homework neatly enough. *Didn't I realize that there was a war brewing in Southeast Asia and I would have to go fight? And how the hell could I fight and kill the enemy if I had sloppy penmanship?* I was only twelve years old and didn't quite know where Southeast Asia was, but was fairly certain my mother wouldn't let me go there. Also, I didn't realize that you had to sign something before you killed someone. I remember that I told her all of this. I also remember that the whacking on the head got harder. I also had to write an essay on respect for my elders. I changed a few of the words around and began the assignment for Mrs. Finch.

I am about halfway through the essay when Mike sticks his head through the door.

"What did she do to you?"

"Essay," I say holding it up. "And I have to sit in the corner for the rest of the afternoon."

"My God, what a heartless old bitch. I'm surprised she didn't take away your milk and cookies."

Oh, God. He is beginning to become a person. He is even trying to have a sense of humor. We banter back and forth for a few more seconds before he heads off to a pharmacology class.

I finish my essay and begin to get bored. Alone in an office I do what every other person before me has done. I snoop. I do not have to look very long before hitting some juicy information. The class ranking.

I am ranked number one both academically and clinically.

"Liver rounds this Friday at the Candlelight," coos Mary Jo Something-orother, a perennial student nurse with nothing but marrying a doctor on her mind. Liver rounds are an ancient ritual whereby nurses and doctors get together in a dark smoky bar near the hospital and get drunk. Usually they start around five in the afternoon, and the real champs don't fall from grace until two or three in the morning.

Female student nurses are particularly welcomed at liver rounds due to their enchantment with physicians. Nurses that have been practicing for a few years don't go near anything with an MD after his name. It appears that they know something that the others don't.

Liver rounds inevitably turn into a major psychodrama: Nurses being groped by doctors. Nurses groping back. Mad dashes back to the hospital to find an empty on-call room or vacant stretcher. Nurses left behind get teary eyed or belligerent.

I decide to go to liver rounds against my better judgment. Get a couple of vodkas into some of the residents, and they get loose with their money. I make it a personal goal never to buy more than one drink, but never leave sober.

The docs don't really know what to do with me. All they really want is a semiconscious girl to fondle. I have noticed that all the gay MDs are living with other MDs. Home must be hell when someone gets sick. Men are the world's biggest babies when they're ill, and physicians just tend to be adolescent by nature.

I come to the conclusion that doctor-nurse marriages are strictly limited to the heterosexual community.

I am thinking these deep and profound thoughts as Myles Lambert, rich, good-looking, and married attempts to bring me into the conversation, which so far has consisted of who has seen the biggest mucus plug.

"What do you say, Steele?"

This man went to Harvard.

"I don't know. What do you say, Lambert?"

In medicine it is assumed that your parents never meant for your first name to be taken seriously.

"How about going up to the bar and getting all of us another round. My treat."

"Swell."

There are only four of us at the Candlelight so far. However, it is still early. Seated at the table, outside of myself and the doctor, are Barbara Smythe, a nice, innocuous girl with big bazooms, and Sister Helen, a tight-lipped over-the-hill nun trying to make sense out of Vatican II. I think I notice that Myles smiles at me a little too much as I take the ten from his hand. I have only had my first Scotch and am in control.

I go over to the bar and place the order. I am drinking, as I always do, Dewars on the rocks. Myles is doing straight vodka tonight. Barbara is drinking beer. And the good sister is having her usual Manhattan.

I return with the drinks and Myles pats my butt in appreciation. I decide that this is going to be an interesting night after all.

"Thanks for the reinforcement," I say as I lift up my glass.

"No problem buddy." This comes from the man that pushes me out of his way to get to the cafeteria.

Barbara is desperately shaking her ample bosom in Myles direction. She is puckering and pursing her lips, and trying to say something intelligent. Myles is staring directly at me.

"Excuse me, doctor." Barbara croons.

"Myles," he corrects.

She gulps for air. "Oh, Myles. Yes, how nice. Excuse me, Myles, but there are several things that I do not understand."

"Such as?"

"Well, such as," Barbara seems at a loss for words. I let my right leg accidentally touch Myles' leg.

"Sorry about that," I lie.

"Nothing to be sorry about," he says as he grabs my other leg. I am being groped by the best of them.

"How's it going, Sister?" I decided that confusing everyone is the best strategy at this point.

"Fine," says Sister Helen just before she pukes on the table.

"It must be the religious training," I say to Myles.

"Must be."

Barbara, the never-ending angel of mercy leads Sister Helen back to the dorm to sleep it off. It is only seven-thirty.

Myles and I are alone. Heh-heh.

"Let's go screw," I say.

He nods.

We leave.

The rest of junior year of nursing school turns out to be interesting. I am seeing Peter the waiter and planning on setting up housekeeping should he ever mention it even slightly. I am also seeing Myles, rich and powerful doctor to the sick, and would run the other way screaming at the top of my lungs if he ever suggested live-in bliss. I am somehow beginning to understand what all the more experienced nurses know about doctors. I do not quite understand what it is yet, but I do know that it is something strange.

Another funny thing begins to happen to me by the end of the school year. Carmella is the one to notice it. I am scared shitless.

Carmella and I are sitting in my room playing Parcheesi and doing shots of Southern Comfort out of plastic medicine cups. A smoldering cigarette dangles from the center of Carmella's mouth.

"So what was your last rotation before becoming the big-time senior?"

"Peds," I answer.

Carmella stares up at me.

"It was fine. No big deal. Just a bunch of sick kids." I knock back another 30cc of Comfort.

"You went through three months of taking care of sick kids and I didn't hear a word of bull out of you?" She stares at me for an answer.

I suddenly feel uncomfortable because I cannot come up with a wise-crack.

"No big deal."

"So you liked it?"

"Yea, I guess. Maybe this nursing thing is going to be all right after all."

"Holy shit," she says. "So what floor did you work on most of the time?"

"Oncology."

"Double holy shit," she says and downs another shot.

It is summer once again, but this year we are given a full four weeks off. The annual convention of hospital sweatshop owners must be coming to town. I am beginning to examine my life. I will be a full-fledged registered nurse in just another year. I begin to think about all the material I will have to know for my state boards. I begin to have anxiety over something that is over a year away. I decide I need a break from all of it.

I call Peter. He wants to see me. Oh good. He has something to tell me he says. Oh God.

Peter and I meet at the Glory Hole. It is a beautiful summer night. The air is warm, clear, and dark. Even Yonkers feels exciting. I decide that Peter is going to ask me to move in. We have been dating heavily for a year now.

I am sitting at the bar sipping a Dewar's and soda, my summer drink. Bernie the bartender is shaking up an umbrella drink for the drag queen at the other end. She is desperately trying to look like a young Bette Davis, but doesn't do much better than a fading Ethel Merman. She winks at me. I wink back. I feel wicked.

Peter walks in and I immediately know that I can forget about any silver patterns.

"Hi," he says as sits down next to me. "A beer please, Bernie."

"What's up?" I say and regret it at the same time. What the hell am I doing making it easy for him? The nurse in me has slipped out. Dammit.

Peter sips his beer and I can see big round sweat rings forming on his shirt. Good.

"I think I can't see you again."

"Vision problem?"

Peter just looks at me.

"No. I mean, I think we should break up."

"Oh."

I am silent. What the hell am I suppose to say—gee, that sounds like a swell idea!?

"What I mean to say is, I have decided to enter the priesthood, and won't be able to see you again."

Jilted for Jesus.

"Peter, you will excuse me if I do not fully understand this. We have been going out for over a year. I have spent many nights in your apartment. We have spent numerous weekends together. On Sundays you always slept in. You don't own a crucifix or a Bible. I don't even know what religion you are! So how the hell do you go from point A to point B!?"

I, of course, have screamed this out loud enough for the Bette Davis cum Ethel Merman wannabe to get overly excited. She is slightly staggering down the bar toward me on platform shoes.

"I can't explain it."

I stand up and order another drink. "Well you better come up with something. Even a good lie at this point would be appreciated. I'll be right back."

I charge pass the teetering queen and head for the men's room. I stop. I think. I call Myles.

A woman answers. Great.

I return to the bar to find Peter gone, and a diluted Ethel sitting in his seat.

"Can mama buy you a drink and make it all better?"

Swell.

I never hear from Peter again. I wonder if altar boys are safe. The rest of my vacation is spent between long days in the medical library studying and long nights at the Glory Hole drinking. I think I have finally found my calling. Science and booze. After all it is just chemistry with a kick.

It is the night before the start of my final year of nursing school. My mother calls me and asks the same old question over the phone. As she whines over the phone I question the sanity of advanced communication technology. Mothers did not bitch as much I bet when they had to resort to the use of smoke signals.

"Why a nurse?" she whines. "You have the brains. You could have been a doctor."

I hear this all the time from my mother, from physicians, from other nurses, from strangers. They actually think that they are paying me a compliment. They have no concept that the remark is rude and stupid.

"Ma," I whine back. "I want to be a nurse, and not a doctor. I like nursing."

She sounds almost tearful. "But why?"

But why, I think to myself. Why, because you didn't give me a goddamn penny for my education and I have been supporting myself since I was eighteen. That's a good reason. But, I don't say this, I am a good son.

"Look we have been over this before. I told you. Nursing is different. It lets you really help people. I get to make a real difference in how people live their lives."

My mother remains doubtful. You would think that I had chosen to live a life of prostitution. Actually, it would probably be more profitable.

I decide not to go over this well-worn conversation and change subjects. Smooth operator am I.

"So, Ma, how are things with the Ava Maria Guild?"

The final year of school is the hardest. We are set free. The instructors simply stand around and drink coffee all day waiting for each us to make a mistake. *You won't have us around forever, you know. You have got to learn to do these things on your own.*

Great. So they simply throw us up on all these different wards and jump on our backs the second we screw up. They call it "transition." I call it the final stage of hell.

You'll thank me for this some day, they tell us. I have never thanked anyone who ever said that to me.

"Mr. Steele, just what in the world do you think you are doing?" demands Mrs. Hesse, an instructor of advanced years but not of thinking.

I stare at Mr. Dennette's exposed rear end and the enema tube in my hand.

"I was just about to give Mr. Dennette his soap suds enema for his surgery tomorrow." Mr. Dennette looks up at me embarrassed. He is only forty two and not in the habit of mooning people while casual conversation is taking place.

"Are you sure that's what you're doing Mr. Steele?" Mrs. Hesse demands once again.

I look at my patient's butt and the enema tube once again. Since I have no intention of chug-a-lugging the concoction in the bag I nod yes.

"Are you positive, young man?"

Mr. Dennette farts and his face turns the color of blood.

"Oh for Christ's sake lady, what the hell do you think he is doing? Watering the petunias?" Mr. Dennette says.

Mrs. Hesse's face forms into twelve perfect horizontal lines.

"Well, I never," she huffs.

"That's probably a big part of your problem, lady." Mr. Dennette says.

She leaves in a righteous huff.

We laugh.

I am in my final rotation before graduation learning how to be a "charge nurse" on a floor. The charge nurse is the one who handles all the doctors' orders and nurses' assignments. You become the supervisor of the floor. Usually, the charge nurse doesn't take a patient assignment, but sometimes has to if staffing is low. It is a lot of work and responsibility without any benefits. No extra pay. No extra time off. No nothing. It is supposed to make you a better person. You have to be a charge nurse if you ever want to become a head nurse.

I am in charge on Ward 55, a forty-bed male medicine floor that is filled with homeless men with multiple diagnoses. A typical patient is a male in his late forties with a history of alcoholism, diabetes, hypertension, liver cirrhosis, and leg ulcers that are infected with dirt and bugs. These guys are sick. I love them.

The head nurse of Ward 55 is Miss Leatice. I do not know her first name. No one calls her anything but Miss Leatice. Silence falls over any room that she walks into, and doctors and nurses stand at attention. If Miss Leatice says something is to be done it will be done, or she will have your ass. She never speaks above a whisper, she is jet black with stark white hair, and is the only female nurse I know that doesn't wear a cap. She is my hero.

It is my first day at charge duty and I don't know what to do. The nurses' station is crowed with nurses, students, and physicians all going through charts and talking. I am standing around looking and feeling foolish. I feel a wave of anxiety come over me. I am going to be responsible for the running of this ward for nearly four weeks. Lives are being entrusted to me. Jesus, I am only a kid, doesn't anyone know this?

Miss Leatice walks in and order automatically kicks in. I breathe a sigh of relief. She takes off her coat.

"Good morning ladies and gentlemen."

Good mornings are muttered back.

"Okay Steele, begin."

I look at her. My face is a blank.

"Sit down child and take report so that the night shift can get their weary butts home."

"Well, I never have taken report on an entire floor before. Today is my first day—what do I do?" I feel myself turn red. The doctors and nurses begin to snicker.

"The first thing you do is stop plucking my nerves." Miss Leatice says in her soft, controlled voice. "Now sit and take report."

I do, but do not have the slightest idea what the hell I am doing. Welcome to the real world. By the end of report my shirt is soaked through with sweat. It is only 7:30 a.m.

Miss Leatice, Miss Fowler, the night charge nurse, and I make the rounds of each patient's room after report. We come to one of our regulars. Mr. Sam Wallen Jr. has been admitted to Ward 55 eighty-seven times in the last two years for alcohol-related disorders. Also, whenever he gets tired of living out of a dumpster he comes for a visit. Junior, as everyone calls him, is one of the more infamous patients we have.

"Good morning, Junior," I say. Miss Leatice slaps the back of my head hard.

"What did you just say?" she snaps.

Stunned, I turn to her and repeat it.

"Let's get one thing straight from the get go. All of the patients on my ward are addressed as mister. No first naming it. No last naming it. You treat each and every one like the Pope. Got it, Steele?"

I nod. Junior smiles at me and waves. He looks like Humpty Dumpty with a tube up his nose.

"Excuse me. Good morning, Mr. Wallen."

"Much better."

When we are between rooms I stop Miss Leatice. "How come he is a mister and I am just a last name?"

"You're just a nurse."

We move on.

I am in my final week of charge rotation. In just seven days I will be a full-fledged nurse. Now I can honestly start really worrying about taking my state licensing boards.

Miss Leatice and I are almost good friends. I have found her weakness—the patients. Her "angels" as she calls them. Miss Leatice truly loves these men. She thinks each and every one of them to be a special gift from God, and cannot understand anyone that doesn't.

It is now 7:45 on Thursday morning. Just two more shifts before I take finals and graduate. I am feeling pretty cocky. Mike and I are going out after we are off duty and get ripped. He says he wants to see what a gay bar looks like from the inside. Why, I say, you been staring at one from the outside?

Miss Leatice and I are leaning against the breakfast cart. Nurses are scurrying up and down the hall giving out the morning trays.

"Nurses shouldn't have to do that," I say pointing to a woman who has the education and licensure as a registered professional nurse and is functioning like a waiter.

"You bet," Miss Leatice responds.

"But they do it anyway."

"You bet."

Miss Jimmi, better known as "Lightening," comes up to us. Lightening was awarded her nickname because of her profound lack of speed or interest in the patients. She is a nurse's aide in a very powerful union. Lightening takes great pride in telling everyone of her very bad heart condition, which forces her to hide in the linen closet at the first mention of work. She isn't going to have no heart attack over some sick person. There is nothing to do but live with her.

"Miss Leatice . . ." Lightening ventures.

"Not now Lightening. Steele and I are in the midst of deep philosophical conversation."

Miss Leatice and I go back to our discussion on nurses performing non-nursing functions.

"Well who do you expect to give these good folks their breakfast? The doctors?"

"Why not?" I shrug.

"Now Steele, not even you . . ."

"Miss Leatice," Lightening interrupts.

"Not now," snaps Miss Leatice.

Lightening slowly closes her mouth and steps back. She has finally learned her lesson.

"Physicians are just as capable with carrying meal trays as nurses. I'm sure that they would do a fine job," I say.

Miss Leatice snorts.

"Excuse me, but . . ."

We both stare Lightening down.

"Oh for God's sake, Steele, where is your sense of reality!"

"Miss . . ."

"Cryin' out loud! What the hell do you want?" Miss Leatice shouts for the very first time. I just stare at Lightening.

Slowly and with great deliberation she speaks.

"You know that new patient in 5522?"

We nod.

"He ain't breathing."

For the first and only time in her career as a nurse's aide Lightening is right.

The death of the patient in 5522 bonds Miss Leatice and I in a strange way. She says she will be at my graduation. I am thrilled.

During the two weeks between the end of my clinical rotation and final exams Carmella and I spend nearly the entire time together. She stays with me around the clock grilling me for finals. No matter where we go she is asking me questions.

"What is the major cause of thyroid storm?"

I dunno.

"How many cc's equal an ounce?"

I dunno.

Diagram fetal circulation.

No way.

And on it goes.

I pass all my finals with flying colors. Miss Finch tells me that I ranked number one in the entire class. I am excited.

"Does that mean I can give a speech at graduation?" I'll show my mother.

"Why of course not. The graduation speech is always given by one of the girls."

Oh.

It is ten minutes before graduation. I peek out into the auditorium. I can see my mother. She has dressed herself in so much purple double-knit polyester that she is actually having a difficult time remaining in her seat. I also see Myles. He is sitting with his new wife. He spots me. He waves. Peter is off in an abbey somewhere. I want to puke.

The band is tuning up and getting ready to play "Pomp and Circumstance." I look at the entire class, all nervous and chattering. We are all in our white uniforms for the very first time. I am moved. We have made it. We are now nurses.

Miss Finch approaches me from behind.

"Richard," she says.

I turn.

"Richard, I am afraid that I have bad news."

I just stare at her. She has never called me by my first name.

"Miss Leatice won't be coming to graduation."

I just look at her.

"I know how much you liked her."

Lik*ed?*

"She's dead. Killed herself by trying to induce an abortion. Bled out in the ER just a few minutes ago."

We are both silent for a very long time.

Miss Finch finally cracks a smile.

"Well, these things happen. Now go out there and smile. You've earned it!"

She turns and leaves.

Welcome to nursing.

PART TWO

"I'm sorry Mr. Steele," Miss Paretsky pouts as she blows out cigarette smoke from here nose like a dragon. "But there simply aren't any positions for a diploma nurse available." I stare at her filterless Camel and watch as she flicks tobacco off her tongue.

"What?"

She slowly shakes her head from side to side. I notice for the first time that she has no neck, just folds of fat that somehow turn into breast globs.

"Nope. Not a one," she says as she flips through a series of index cards.

"You mean in this entire hospital there isn't one opening for a nurse on any shift, on any ward?" I am incredulous. I know she is wrong.

Miss Paretsky throws her head back slightly and laughs. "Oh my, yes. There are plenty of openings, but we don't want to hire diploma nurses any more." She leans forward and smiles. "We only want nurses with a bachelor's degree." Her grin broadens. Her teeth are dark yellow from years of smoking Camels.

"Miss Paretsky, I just spent three years of my life at this very hospital going to your very own diploma school. Not only that but I had a full scholarship. And I graduated first in my class. Now you tell me after all of that my education is not good enough to get a job here?"

"We want baccalaureate nurses, Mr. Steele."

"Why the hell didn't somebody tell me that three years ago!"

"There is no need to curse me out young man," she says as she stands up. "Our nursing school is one of the finest in the country, but we need nurses with bachelor's degrees. I think our interview is over."

"Well, what am I suppose to do?"

"I would suggest that you go back to school."

"Back? I just got out."

"Good-bye, Mr. Steele."

I get up and start to leave. As I am nearing the office door I can hear Mrs. Paretsky mumble to her secretary. The only words I can make out are "homo little shit."

"Carmella, no one will hire me." I lament over beer and cigarettes.

"Sounds like lots of employers are exercising good judgment."

"Don't be a shit."

"Sorry. It's my training."

"Five different hospitals tell me the same thing. They only want someone with a bachelor's degree. What am I going to do?"

"Get one."

There is only one university in the area that offers a bachelor's of nursing degree. I apply for admission. I am accepted but do not go. They will give me one semester of credit for my three years in nursing school. I am sure that the admissions counselor is wrong. Oh no, he says. Diploma nursing education doesn't count for much. I would have to start from scratch.

I have until the end of summer to move out of my dorm room. I take a job piercing ears one afternoon a week in a local jewelry store. Not bad pay. Ten bucks a person, or five a lobe.

I am sitting at the Glory Hole trying to make sense out of three years of grueling education and my current employment at a jewelry store. No one is bothering me. I am casting off definite "do-not-approach" vibrations. I also have a huge splatter of blood down the front of my shirt.

Bernie buys me a drink on the house and I rummage around for a cigarette. Bernie gets one out of his pack from under the bar and lights it then hands it to me.

"Tough day?"

"I've had better."

"From the looks of you so did your patient."

Bernie is staring at the blood. He thinks I have a real job, saving real lives. I cannot explain to him that the reason for the blood is that a crazed mother stormed into the jewelry shop and caught me piercing her beloved daughter's ears. With the rationale that only a mother could possibly understand she ripped the needle out of my hands causing me to slice her daughter's ear. Blood flew everywhere. The girl started screaming and the mother started hollering. After all was calm the poor kid had half an earlobe hanging and had to be taken to an emergency room to have it stitched. The mother just stared at me for the demon in white that I am. I am certainly glad this woman wasn't around to object to my circumcision.

I am about to lie to Bernie when Carmella walks in.

"I figured my favorite homosexual angel of mercy might be here repairing his damaged spirit." Carmella eyes my blood-stained shirt. "What the hell did you do to yourself?"

"I'm fine. But there is a fourteen-year-old girl with a newly acquired resemblance to Dumbo who is probably pissed off."

"It certainly doesn't sound like something that is going to go down in the history books."

"That depends on who writes the history."

"Never mind all that." She silently signals Bernie for a drink. "I come as the bearer of glad tidings. You have a real nursing job!"

Carmella takes a piece of paper out of her pocket and waves it in the air.

"I stopped by your dorm room looking for you and I found this note taped to your door. So I naturally took it down and read it."

"I wouldn't have it any other way."

"I know that."

My respirations are increasing. She is toying with me.

"Perhaps you would like to read it."

I grab the letter from her hands and rip it open. It reads:

"Dear Mr. Steele,

There appears to be an opening on the night shift in pediatrics. I doubt that you will be interested in this, but I was asked to offer it you from the head nurse. I am not sure why. If you care for this position be in my office by nine tomorrow." It is unsigned.

"She didn't sign it. What if this is a trick?"

"Honey, the only tricks around here are the gentlemen at the bar."

I am at the nurse recruiter's office at 8:45 a.m. I knock and go in. She doesn't look up from her *Daily News*. All I can see is a bobbing head and billows of cigarette smoke.

"So you want the job. It yours. Don't ask me why, but the head nurse wanted you. Report tomorrow at seven a.m. for two days of clinical orientation and then the head nurse will schedule you. Your starting salary, without a bachelor's degree, is $10,050."

"How much would it have been with a degree?"

"$10,300."

I spend the night alone in my room ironing my uniform and polishing my shoes. I feel just like Hazel. At 10 p.m. I am in bed but cannot sleep. I have a real job, making real money. Also, I won't have to move. I can stay in the dorm. I also put my name on the waiting list for one of the hospital's studio apartments.

I arrive on the ward at 6:45 a.m. I am the whitest creature on earth. I fell like an overzealous Good Humor man. Miss Jones, the head nurse, is there counting narcotics with the night charge nurse. She totally ignores me until she is done accounting for every last pill and vial.

Slowly she turns to me. "Mr. Steele, welcome. I, as you know, am Miss Jones, your new head nurse." She attempts a smile but fails and shakes my hand.

"Now, what you don't know, Mr. Steele, is that I don't like you."

My throat is totally dry and tight.

"Please do not get me wrong," she continues. How could I possibly misinterpret her statement?

"I have nothing against you personally. I don't even know you. I just do not think that men should be allowed in nursing. And I feel, as I'm sure you also know, that men in nursing are usually . . ." she is searching for a word, probably the most damning. "I think most male nurses are . . . sissies!"

I do not know what to do. I do the first foolish thing that comes into my head. I speak.

"Thank you for making me feel welcome Miss Jones. I'm sure I couldn't have asked for a nicer beginning."

"Oh don't be so sensitive."

"Oh, pardon my sensitivity. I think it was something that I was taught in nursing school. Let me ask you something. Would you have said that you didn't like black people if I was black?"

"Well, of course not! What kind of person do you think I am!?"

"One of the world's biggest assholes for starters. You see, Miss Jones, I'm gay; not a sissy. Why the hell did you hire me in the first place?"

"You just swore at me!"

"I did."

"I could fire you."

"You could."

"You don't care?"

"I don't."

She just stares through me. I stare right back. How the hell do I get involved with these kinds of people?

"Mr. Steele, I am not going to fire you."

"I know."

Her eyebrows knit into a grotesque caterpillar shape. "How do you know?"

"You must have hired me for a reason. No normal person would hire someone they didn't like without a reason. And I am giving you the benefit of being normal, just because it's my first day and all."

Miss Jones' face brightens. "Well, you are clever Mr. Steele."

"Well?"

"Well what?" She turns to go away. "Oh the reason."

"Yes. The reason."

"To lift! My girls are just exhausted from all the lifting and pulling of the children and stretchers. I thought a good strong man would help my nurses."

Carmella and I are sitting in our usual seats at the Glory Hole. I have just finished my first day as a graduate nurse and am feeling miserable. The encounter with Miss Jones soured the entire day. The other staff nurses told me not to worry, it was just her way. She really didn't mean anything by it. She was just a little hyper, but really very nice. I smiled and nodded appreciatively all day but retained my doubts.

"She must be some bitch," Carmella says as she pops open a new box of Marlboros.

"I guess I was expecting a female version of Mr. Rogers as my first head nurse. Believe me this wasn't any lovely day in the neighborhood. All she did all day was arrange my schedule so that I am on every night there is surgery scheduled for the morning. I figure she expects me to lift and cart all the kids off to the operating room before my shift is over. How in the hell am I to learn anything if all I am doing is hauling kids to surgery?"

"Steele, I am sure that the other night nurses do not expect that of you."

"Then how come they all came up to me and felt my arm muscles and smiled. I swear, I felt like the main course at a cannibal convention."

"You never mind when I feel your muscles," pipes in Bernie.

"We are talking different muscles."

"So how are you going to handle her?"

I stop and think. The first sign of maturity.

"I am going to be a good nurse."

"Oh, that ought to kill her."

It is 5 a.m. and I am standing in the medication room preparing all the pre-op injections that I will give before getting the kids off to the OR. I read, then reread, each order carefully. Giving narcotics to kids gives me the willies. I calculate each dose and carefully draw it up into a syringe labeled with each patient's name and ID number.

I notice that Mary, the nurse that was floated from a medical floor to help me out, looks a bit woozy. Staying awake and working all night is a very strange thing indeed, but I have adapted well. My years of a bar carousing do not go unrewarded.

With my attention diverted to Mary's level of consciousness I realize that I have two unlabeled syringes in front of me.

"Shit."

"What's wrong?" slurs Mary.

"I wasn't paying attention and I got these medications mixed up. I don't know who gets what." I say as I look at the syringes for an answer.

"No problem," Mary brightens out of her semi-stupor. "Let me see the syringes."

I point to the two unmarked syringes.

"Just as I thought," chuckles Mary. "Both medications are clear."

"Yea. So?"

"So, it doesn't matter who gets what as long as they are both clear."

I am astounded.

"You don't really believe that?"

"Believe? Honey, I know. I've been a nurse for nearly twenty years."

"But Mary, one of these injections is for six-month-old baby and the other is for a two-year-old. The dosage is dramatically different. The med for the two-year-old could kill the baby."

"Bullshit."

Mary walks away.

I waste both syringes down the sink and start over.

It is 6:15 a.m. Mary is nowhere to be found. But who is looking? All my pre-op medications have been given correctly, and I have killed no one. I go to the kitchen to make a fresh pot of coffee for the day shift that will be in soon. An unwritten rule of nursing on nights: Always make the day shift happy. So I make them coffee.

Ernie, a very overly ambitious and underly intelligent third-year medical student is standing in the kitchen looking through the cupboards.

"Can I help you with anything?" I say, letting my officious nursing temper come up to the surface. He makes my whites bristle.

Startled Ernie turns around. "What? No. I'm sorry. I was just looking for some breakfast. I didn't have time to go to the cafeteria."

"It's only six fifteen, you have forty-five minutes before report begins."

"I know," he says sheepishly. "But, I wanted to review a few charts. You know, so I look good."

I know. I go about the business of making coffee while Ernie continues his search for food. As the coffee is brewing I leave Ernie to his quest as I go prepare for report. I want to look good too.

At 6:45 I go back into the kitchen to get a cup of coffee. Ernie is sitting there eating oatmeal out of an emesis basin. I am startled.

"Where did you get that?"

"The oatmeal? Oh, I found some in the back of the top closet."

"Not the oatmeal. The basin."

"From that room across the hall."

"Was it wrapped or unwrapped?"

"Umm . . . it was unwrapped. I couldn't find a bowl and I thought this would do. I didn't want to use a new one."

"Ernie, that is a vomit bucket you're eating out of."

"Oh, I know that. I figured that they are sterilized so what's the big deal."

"The dirty ones are unwrapped, that's the big deal."

I finish report and make rounds with Miss Jones.

"Mary says you were a little abrupt with her last night Mr. Steele."

"I don't recall being abrupt."

"She was trying to give you the value of her experience as a nurse in medication administration, I believe."

"Her experience would have killed someone."
"Now, Mr. Steele, really. This is a hospital. No one kills anyone here."

It is noon. I am asleep after a long shift. The phone rings. It is Mike
Wolfe. Somehow we have become friends.
"Steele, you are never going to guess what I just heard."
I groan. Mike has recently started working day shift on the male correc-
tional unit. A good place for a nice straight boy. Gay porno in the making, if
you ask me.
"Mike, do I call you at four o'clock in the morning?"
"No, but you could."
"Ah, the excitement of potential."
I nod off back to sleep.
"Sister Helen has been made new house supervisor," Mike says jolting me
awake.
"What?!" I am now up. "The puking nun is now a supervisor?!"
"The one and the same."
"How the hell did this happen? She just graduated with us. My God, she
has been a nurse for only four months, and now she is house supervisor."
"She's sleeping with the new nursing director."
"They never should have let them out of their habits."
"I agree."

Patty O'Malley is giving me report from the evening shift. She is the kind
of nurse I hate and hope to be. She is always pristine and smelling vaguely
like springtime. Her mannerisms are letter perfect. She never picks her
nose. All of her charting is done in pained but perfect Catholic handwriting
that details every aspect of each of her patients. She never calls in sick. I hate
her. I want to be her. Never.
"In room 402 is Johnnie Whitter, six months old, failure to thrive. He's
been here now for a total of six weeks. His weight is up three ounces from
last week which is a good sign. I find that if you sing to him while trying to
give him the bottle his sucking reflex is stronger. Try and feed him in small
amounts every two hours. I also spoke with his mother again tonight. It appears we have a lot of teaching to do. She says she didn't feed him at home
because he stops crying. She thought he was happy."
"Happy?"

"She didn't understand that babies need to eat even when they don't cry. No crying, no food."

"So he became too weak to cry and she still didn't feed him because she assumed he was happy. After all he wasn't crying. So he comes to us looking like a raisin with legs and arms. God, I hope he makes it."

"So do I, but it is still real shaky," says Patty.

"The next patient in room 403 is Dickey Hallan. He is a sixteen-year-old with end-stage leukemia."

"End stage?"

"Yea. They only give him another three months."

"Oh God. Does he know?"

"They always know. But if you mean has he been told? The answer is no. His dad doesn't want him to know."

I look away from Patty. I didn't expect a general pediatric unit to be like this. Now babies don't eat and teenagers lay dying.

After report is over I read Dickey Hallan's chart and go over his lab work. He won't live more than sixty days. His whole body is about to shut down. God, could I use a drink.

I walk into Dickey's room with his midnight medication. He is lying in bed asleep. He reminds me of a great big beached whale, all bloated and pale. I stare at him. Beneath all the swelling I can see a kid, or what is left of one.

I quietly count his respirations and check his pulse before I put his medication in the IV His eyes flicker open as the two fluids combine.

"Who are you?" he asks.

"Your night nurse. My name is Steele."

"That's a funny name."

"It's my last name, but everyone calls me by it."

"Do you have a first name?"

"It's Richard. The same as yours."

"Now I know why everyone calls you Steele."

He closes his eyes and appears to drift off to sleep. I finish administering the medication. As I begin to leave the room he stirs.

"Steele?"

I turn.

"Am I dying?"

I pause for just a moment. "Yes, you are."

"I thought so."

He turns over onto his left side and pulls the covers over his head.

"Goodnight."
"Goodnight."

I have three days off and I decide to become healthy. I will take water in my scotch, smoke only low-tar cigarettes, and use margarine instead of butter. That should do it. Also, I vow to do 100 sit-ups—sometime in my life. There is a familiar knock on my door as I make my health resolutions while getting dressed.

"Who's there?"

"June Cleaver!"

"June, what the fuck are you doing out of the house? Where's Wally? What's happened to the Beaver?"

"Wally is with Eddie snorting coke and the Beaver is with Lumpy popping zits." Carmella sweeps into the room holding a shoe box at arm's length.

"Now Mrs. Cleaver where are your chiffon and pearls?"

"Ward wears them on alternating Fridays." Carmella rips open the shoe box. "Here, have a brownie."

I take one and bite into it.

"These taste like shit!"

"Why yes they do, but they are also laced with tons of marijuana." Carmella pops an entire brownie into her mouth.

"Actually," I say, taking a second brownie, "they are not so bad." I smack my lips. "Not bad at all."

We consume four brownies and a six-pack of beer each before we head out the door to go have dinner and hit the Glory Hole.

We are sitting in a dirty Howard Johnson's looking at the menus.

"How do you feel?" I ask.

"I feel fine. How do you feel?"

"Fine. Not stoned at all."

"Me neither."

"I guess those grass brownies take awhile to hit you."

"I guess."

A waitress approaches. She is dangerously lanky with the disturbing name of Candy. Carmella and I continue to stare at our menus.

"They have about four-thousand items listed here." Carmella is speaking through rapid inhalations.

"It is all very interesting." I drawl out as I read the menu like it was the Holy Grail.

"I think so too."

I stare at Carmella breathing. I am transfixed.

"Whaddawant?" Candy demands as she slops glasses of water in front of us.

I cannot move. I cannot speak.

"You okay honey?"

"We're just fine and dandy," pipes in Carmella.

"So, whaddahave," growls Candy.

I attempt speech but find that my tongue is permanently affixed to the roof of my mouth. Carmella flicks a cigarette into her mouth and lights it blowing out a steady jet stream of smoke. She tilts her head back and moans.

"Lobster," she says as she sucks deeply on her cigarette. "We will have two of the finest lobster dinners that your chef can prepare."

I say nothing.

"Honey, this here is a Howard Johnson's. You know, ice cream, burgers, coffee."

"You have lobster on your menu."

"Well, yea, but no one ever orders it."

"And a bottle of your finest white wine. A nice California Chardonnay would be peachy."

"Honey, the only thing peachy around here is the busboy. I'll bring you our finest screw-capped jug wine. I'm sure it will go well with your lobster."

Candy leaves.

"We're just a couple swells," I say before I pass out on the Formica.

I wake up in the Glory Hole. Carmella has me propped up in a chair at the bar.

"Did I enjoy the lobster?"

"Every last morsel."

"Do I want a drink?"

"I'm sure you do."

"Good."

Dickey's father is waiting for me as I get off the elevator the next night.

"Are you the one who told my son?"

I can see the distant, once-familiar resemblance.

"Yes. I guess I am."

"What I really want to do is punch you in the face," Mr. Hallan says in very measured tones. I wait for him to continue. "But Dickey wants to talk to you. He says he has some questions."

"I'll be right in."

I move down the hall toward the nurses' station.

"Mr. Hallan," I say as I turn around. "I'm sorry."

"Well, he was bound to figure it out anyway."

"What I mean is I'm sorry that your son is dying. I really am."

Mr. Hallan's chest heaves just once before the tears start to flow.

"Oh God. So am I." He cries.

I walk back to him. "Why don't we talk first?"

My first conversation with Mr. Hallan lasts for more than an hour. He shows up every night around 2 a.m. after I am done checking on the kids and giving out the midnight medications. We talk. He holds Dickey. He cries when we are alone. Mrs. Hallan cannot come to the hospital to watch her son die. She is in a nursing home with irreversible brain damage from a car accident. I do not know anything about Dickey's two younger sisters.

"How are your girls doing?"

He looks startled.

"I guess they're okay. I don't know. I think I've forgotten about them. They just always appear to be healthy, and I don't have time for that anymore."

I pour him another cup of coffee. We are standing in the kitchen of the ward.

"They're important too."

"Yes, I know." He looks heavy.

"I guess I haven't been a very good father to them for a long time."

"I think you have been the best father that you can be at this time. They know what you are going through because they are going through it too. I'm working the evening shift this Saturday. Why don't you bring them in after eight and the four of us can talk."

"You know, I haven't even told them about Dickey yet. I keep on saying that its some bad blood disease. They know about their mother of course, but . . ."

"Let's find out what they want to know on Saturday. I'll help you tell them if that is what they want. Kids are remarkable in letting you know what they want."

I glance at my watch. "Gotta go Mr. Hallan. It's time for the four a.m. meds, and I want to get at them before Mary volunteers her services."

I start to leave. Mr. Hallan turns and looks out the kitchen window into the clear night sky. Stars shine brightly. He looks up and gulps a sigh that heaves his whole body.

"I'll never get the chance to teach him how to drive."

I know that he is crying. I say nothing. I do not know what to say. I want to cry too, but there are twenty-five kids waiting on me.

I leave.

"Mr. Steele, I want to see you immediately after report," Miss Jones darts.

I groan internally.

"Yes, Miss Jones."

I drag report out slowly for the new med students that are starting their peds rotation. Also, I don't want to speak with Miss Jones any sooner than necessary.

"Now, Mr. Steele," she says after we have made rounds. "It has been brought to my attention that you have allowed, if not in fact, encouraged, a family member to visit the ward after hospital visiting hours."

"Why, yes, Dickey's father."

"Please stop it."

"Miss Jones, Dickey is dying. His father talks to me. He needs to be here as much as he can. Between taking care of his wife and Dickey, he is living in hell and he still has to go to work and take care of his daughters."

"I understand all of that very well, Mr. Steele. I am the head nurse after all, and I have been a nurse longer than you have been alive. However, the hospital policy is very clear on this. Visiting hours are from one to eight. No exceptions."

"What is the hospital policy on dying kids?"

"No exceptions Mr. Steele."

We just stare at each other. It is at this very instant that I decide to ask for a transfer. I love the kids, but this lady is a lunatic. Maybe I am burnt out. I realize that I have been out of school for only eight months. What the hell is happening?

"You will tell him, Mr. Steele, or shall I?"

"I will." I lie as Miss Jones turns and walks away. I never even consider saying anything to Mr. Hallan.

I stop by Dickey's room on the way out. He is sitting in bed. There is blood caked around his nostrils and ears. He has been bleeding for days and we are afraid if we remove the scabs he will start bleeding again. I can smell clotted blood hanging in the air.

"Dickey, do you need the bed pan?"

He just looks at me vacantly. I pull back the covers. Between his legs is fresh blood and stool. He is hemorrhaging out his bowels. I take his pulse. I estimate it is nearly two hundred and very thready. His blood pressure is barely audible. This is it. He is dying.

I kiss him on the forehead.

"That's from your mom and dad."

There is momentary change in his eyes. I swallow hard. It is time for the fireworks to begin. I call for help, and quickly explain his condition to the intern. Within seconds the room is crowed with machines and people. We are trying to save a dying boy from dying so that he can die.

We work on Dickey for two hours putting in tubes, giving blood, compressing his chest, ventilating his lungs, and giving useless medications. I try to touch his body the entire time to let him know that I am there.

"Let's call it," says the intern. There is no hope. Dickey is dead, and everyone in the room is a little dead too.

The medical staff leaves as quickly as they came. I stare down at Dickey. He still reminds me of that beached whale. But now his body has been invaded by every conceivable tube and machine. All lifeless. All useless.

Patty O'Malley is standing behind me and beginning to clean up the room. I do not move. I cannot move.

"He's your first, isn't he?"

I turn my head slightly to her.

"He the first kid you've ever seen die?" She gently asks again looking directly at Dickey.

I shake my head no.

"You were very good to him and his father. You should be proud that you were able to help so much."

I start to cry.

Patty holds me. "It's okay. Cry now, in the next few years you won't be able to anymore."

Miss Jones comes into the room.

"You performed very well in here Mr. Steele."

"Thank you," I mutter.

Miss Jones goes over to Dickey's body and begins removing all the tubes.

"I just want you to be aware that since no official code was called I cannot pay you overtime." Miss Jones snaps an IV line from Dickey's arm and blood still oozes. "That is hospital policy."

"Has anyone called his dad yet?" I say.

I walk out of the room without ever looking back at Dickey.

"Where the fuck do you think his father is," the intern is yelling in the nurses' station. "His son is dead and I can't get him on the fucking phone."

"Try the nursing home. He is probably visiting his wife," I say. "And stop being such an asshole."

"Listen nursey . . ." The intern is ranting about me as I leave.

I am walking out through the lobby when I notice a familiar shape. Mr. Hallan is sleeping in a chair in the corner. He looks peaceful. I do not know what to do. I want to just go out the door, but I can't.

I stand over him until he awakens.

He just stares up at me and says, "He's gone isn't he?"

I nod.

Mr. Hallan slowly gets up and heads toward the elevators. He turns to say something but doesn't. He goes into the elevator. We never see each other again.

I do not go into work that evening or the next. I feel sick. I sit in my room and try to write Mr. Hallan a letter. I start and stop the letter at least a dozen times. I never finish it.

The night is quiet when I do return to work. No one bothers with me. I feel like shit. Dickey's room is still empty and I avoid any contact with it.

My shift is nearly over and I feel exhausted. Thank God I have only four kids to get ready for the OR. Carefully, I prepare the pre-op medications and begin my rounds.

A little girl startles as I walk into her room. She sits up in bed with her eyes wide open. For an instant I feel refreshed.

"Hi there sweetheart. My name is Steele and I am the nurse that is going to help you have your tonsils taken out."

She sucks in all the air her little six-year-old lungs can hold and pouts, and shakes her head from side to side. I know what's next. I've been through this before.

"You don't want your tonsils taken out?"

A definite "no" of the head.

"They hurt you don't they?"

A slight "yes."

I glance down at her name band.

"Janie, as soon as the doctors take them away you won't have that terrible sore throat anymore. You'll just feel a little hoarse for a couple of days and than you can play and yell with your friends. Won't that be better?"

A typical *I guess so* look.

"Okay Janie, I have to give you some medicine that is going to make you feel sleepy so you won't feel the doctor tickling the back of your throat."

"Okay," Janie says suddenly deciding to trust in me.

"The medicine I am going to give you is going to hurt you for a second. I have to give you a shot in your rear end, and it may hurt but just for a second. I promise."

"It's gonna hurt me?"

"Just for a second and then it will go away." I stroke her hair and help turn her over. She is beginning to cry softly. "Janie, it's okay to cry. You can even yell, but promise me you won't move. And if it hurts too much you can punch me in the nose after I'm done. Okay?"

She doesn't speak. I take her silence for consent. With kids you take what ever you can.

I quickly wipe her butt with alcohol and plunge the needle in skillfully. Just as the needle breaks her skin Janie yells:

"SHIIITTTT!!!!!!!!!!!"

I finish the injection.

"Oh shit, oh shit, oh shit!"

I rub the injection site to ease any residual pain.

"Where did you learn to say 'shit' like that Janie?"

"From mommy."

"Well let's strike a deal. Saying words like shit is no big thing, but I do think you should wait until you're a little older and understand what it means."

"Okay. Can I punch you in the nose now?"

"Sure."

I pick Janie up and she takes both of her hands and forms them into fists before slamming my nose between them. Instantly my blood is everywhere. Why did I become a nurse? I could have been a New York City garbageman, making twice as much pay and working in much better surroundings.

I lay Janie back down in her bed and make sure the side rails are up. I leave the room.

"Shit!" I say in the hallway holding my bleeding nose.

"I heard that!"

I am tempted to go back in there and take out her tonsils myself. That thought alone comforts me as I go down the hall to give report.

My child-induced bloody nose grants me much sympathy from everyone and the opportunity to call in sick again. I am not good at being sick. I whine. I moan. I don't understand how come the whole entire world doesn't come to a dead halt because I have the sniffles. I am a typical man.

Women are much better patients than men. It probably has to do with the childbirth experience. The intense pain of childbirth—never mind raising the kid—causes women to tolerate everyday illness. Men, regardless of sexual orientation, are pansies.

My benevolent thoughts about sisterhood are cut short as I lie on my bed and feel my face expand. I have covered my face with a bag of ice but it is not helping much. My nose is beginning to spread from ear to ear.

The phone rings.

"Steele, it's Patty O'Malley. Guess who got fired?"

"Me?" A logical assumption.

"No, asshole. Miss Jones!"

I am shocked. I also cannot breathe.

"You have got to be kidding. Why in the world did they fire her?"

"Who knows? Probably for being a frigid fussbudget."

"Frigidity is an employment criterion?"

"With our nursing director it is."

"Well, I'll never have to worry about being fired for that."

"That is a well-known fact Steele."

I am nonplussed.

"So who is going to be the new head nurse?"

"Oh you are going to love this . . ."

I wait.

"Sister Helen!"

I groan and fall back in my bed. My head is about to implode.

It appears that Sister Helen possesses some magical quality that is not apparent to the rest of the world. She is to be the acting head nurse of the pediatric unit while remaining one of the house supervisors. Patty O'Malley will be "in charge" on a daily basis we are told.

The departure of Miss Jones results in nothing. Everyone acts like nothing happened. The woman had been at the hospital almost twenty years and no one says squat about her being canned. This is my first lesson in nurse survival: everyone is cheerfully expendable.

I am sleeping after working twelve hours. I am exhausted. I have to be back at the hospital by 10:30 p.m. I barely have enough time to get some sleep and eat. The phone rings. I pick it up but remain asleep.

"Mr. Steele, you are to report to the intensive care unit tonight."

The words are being spoken by a fool of a caller, and are not making any real sense to me.

"Mr. Steele, do you hear me? Are you there?"

"I'm here, sort of," I am coming to a vague level of consciousness. "Who the hell is this?"

"Sister Helen." Her voice is ice.

Having just cursed at a nun I know that I am doomed for all eternity.

I try making a quick sign of the Cross and manage to knock a lamp onto the floor causing it to shatter.

"Holy fucker!" I say in a crisp clear voice.

"What did you call me?" Sister Helen's voice bulges on the other end of the phone.

Sitting up I say, "I didn't call you anything. I just broke a lamp." I mean I could not attest to her being holy or a fucker. However, the latter seemed highly likely given her rise to nursing supervisor.

Sister Helen lets me suffer in silence as punishment.

"Let me repeat myself, Mr. Steele. You are to report to the intensive care unit tonight instead of the pediatrics floor. There is a twelve-year-old boy down there with some significant emotional problems and second- and third-degree burns over sixty percent of his body. He will be your patient. The ICU nurses say they don't feel comfortable caring for a child. You are to go down there for two to three nights and make them feel comfortable. Do you have any questions Mr. Steele?"

"Is the kid acute? How fresh are the burns? Is he on a respirator? Do I get any extra pay for working ICU and teaching?"

Sister Helen is more than annoyed.

"Mr. Steele, experience is your reward. Plus, according to hospital policy, a supervisor can assign you to work in any area that needs coverage at her will. So I am putting you in ICU for a few nights." She pauses clearly to regain a respectable level of nunhood. "The child is not acutely ill. The burns are several days old and he was transferred from another hospital to us because he has family in the area."

"How did he get burned?"

"By squirting lighter fluid on a barbecue. The can blew up all over him."

I am nervous about going to the ICU. Critical care nurses are special. They are tough, bitchy, and smart. I wonder what the hell do they need me for.

The ICU is located on the same floor as the OR. Just walking up to the doors of the unit makes me nervous. I haven't been in the ICU since I was in school, and then that was only to observe. We were told that you needed several years of experience to get a job in the unit, and you had to be a damn good nurse. I never thought that I would ever get the chance to be in a unit.

I take a final deep breath and push open the double doors. Inside there are eight beds in a large rectangular room separated by tired-looking curtains. There is only one bed that is completely isolated by glass partitions. To the left is long desk that is supporting mountains of old coffee cups and half-eaten sandwiches together with patients' charts and medical records. My eyes search around for anyone familiar. I do not know anyone. All I see are four nurses frantically doing whatever they are doing. I certainly do not have any idea.

"Are you the guy from peds?" says a voice from my right. I turn to see a very top-heavy nurse stretching every last fiber of her scrubs with her breasts.

"I'm Diana, the night charge nurse," she says, extending her hand. "We are glad you are here." Diana turns sideways and her bosoms follow about two seconds later. I conclude that they must be independent life forms.

"Don't worry about my tits sweetheart. You'll get use to them. Everyone does." She gives them a little push upward. "What is your name, sweetheart?"

"Steele," I say, feeling like a fool.

"Okay Steele, you look real angelic in that white uniform, but in this ICU we wear scrubs. Grab a pair by the OR and go change before we get report."

I have been in ICU for two minutes and have uttered one word and stared at the charge nurse's tits, and have been caught. I am weak. I return to the unit in scrubs with my angel of mercy costume safely rolled up in a paper bag.

Diana and the rest of the nurses are sitting around the station gulping coffee and writing notes, analyzing EKG stripes, and checking blood values. I feel like a kid on my first day of school. Diana mercifully notices me.

"Hey everyone, this is Steele. He's the nurse from peds that is going to take care of our crispy critter."

Everyone looks up at me and groans a hello.

"Honey, don't you mind them. They're just a little cranky because we are working so short down here, and I think the majority of them haven't gotten laid since nursing school."

"I always thought that there was a waiting list to get to be an ICU nurse."

"Waiting list? Are you kidding? I would take anyone that is breathing independently and has half a brain. And wait until you hear the one that is going to give us report. Dumb as a bedpan. But she is a pair of hands, and God we do need them." Diana shifts in her chair and pulls out a chart. "You're going to be here for a few nights. You look around and see if you like it. Maybe, you'll want to transfer down here. We have a lot of fun."

"Oh, I don't have the experience to work in a unit."

"No one does when they first start out. Anyway, we get lots of kids down here, and it would sure be nice having someone who knows what to do with them. Think about it."

"Sure." I would kill to work in the ICU. I just never thought it possible. I figured that all ICU nurses came from heaven or something. I am wrong.

"Okay, who the hell is ready for report?" Karen says.

"That is Karen," explains Diana. "She just came to us from detox, and is a little wild. She is also the one who is a little slow," Diana says without lowering her voice.

"Slow? If she were any slower she would be a stop sign." A male voice booms.

Diana laughs. "This gorgeous hunk of manhood is Harry O'Brien, our one and only baccalaureate nurse in the unit. I think he is supposed to be an inspiration to the rest of us to go back for our degrees. I fear the only inspiration he has generated down here is X-rated. There is not a gal down here that wouldn't get into stirrups for a pelvic by this man." Diana laughs again and pinches his butt.

Before Harry can say anything Karen slams what is left of her body down in the chair in front of me. She runs her hand through her stringy hair and then sniffs it.

"Who the fuck has a cigarette?"

I hand her one of mine.

"Thanks cookie-face. Look, let me give report on my other patient first to Harry so he can go in the supply room and jerk off."

"I don't jerk off." Harry protests, "I pleasure myself."

"Well pardon my masturbation mistake."

Karen leans into an open chart and makes some final notes. I lean back toward Diana.

"You don't even have to ask," says Diana. "Yes, she always talks like that. Even to the patients. Even to her mother. Sort of your basic, 'Hi Ma! How the fuck you doing?' I'm convinced that she is an ex-nun. Who else would talk that way?"

I nod in agreement to Diana, and I return my attention to the report that Karen is giving Harry.

Karen says: "You remember this lady. Forty-two years old with a history of pernicious anemia and pneumonia. She was doing fine. Then all of a sudden she stopped breathing and had to be tubed. She was in the ICU for three or four days postarrest and doing real well, and then all of a sudden went down the toilet."

Harry nods.

"Well, she is still in the toilet. Big time."

Karen goes through each body system and tells Harry what is wrong with this patient. I am impressed. She doesn't sound dumb to me. Diana, on the other hand, just looks over at Karen with a slight squint in her eye. All of a sudden Diana turns to me and asks:

"What do you know about pernicious anemia, Steele?"

"Not much really. We don't see it much in peds. It's a vitamin B_{12} deficiency that can lead to all sorts of neurological problems, and even death if left untreated. However, I always thought that it was fairly treatable. You know, you just give the patient B_{12} shots on a regular basis and they live happily ever after."

"Has she been getting her B_{12} Karen?" Diana asks.

"Don't be such an asshole! Of course, I am making sure that she is getting her B_{12}. In fact we ran out of B_{12} about a week ago, so I doubled some B_6 until the pharmacy restocks."

Harry spits out his coffee all over Karen and jumps up. Diana is frozen with her mouth wide open. Everyone else in the unit was silent.

My eyes were about to bug out of my head.

"You did what?" I manage to say.

"I gave two B_6s until the B_{12} was restocked," Karen stupidly repeats. "What the fuck is the big deal? Everyone knows that six and six are twelve. So why all the big fucking faces?"

"Well Karen," says Diana. "What you don't seem to understand is that B_6 and B_{12} are two entirely different vitamins."

"Oh."

"Apparently, you also do not understand that B_6 does not do the job of B_{12}."

"Oh."

"Also, you apparently do not understand that you are one of the dumbest cunts on the face of the earth."

"Now wait a minute . . ." Karen attempts.

"No. You wait a minute! Because of your stupidity there is a forty-two-year-old woman in an ICU bed half dead. I think you should clean out your locker and meet me down in the nursing office in ten minutes. You are fired." Diana's breasts have heaved up and down on each word.

Karen, blessed with sense for the first time in her life, doesn't say anything. She just gets up and leaves.

Diana turns toward me. "You better be smart."

The ICU scares the hell out of me, but I like it. The scene between Karen and Diana is forever engraved into my mind. I double-check everything before I move. My patient's burns are over ten days old and he is out of the acute phase. His needs are very complex including putting a dressing to his face and chest, and lots of pain medication. There is no way to pull skin off of someone's face without causing a great deal of agony.

Going through his medical history I note that he has been in group homes for the past four years and has a history of drug abuse and truancy.

The psych note on him says that he is "aggressive in his acting out and manipulative." I think back to my last psych experience and start to sweat. Maybe I should premedicate myself before going into his cubicle?

I look at him through the cubicle glass and wave. He has been placed in isolation to protect him from potential infection. He gives me the finger. This is going to be swell. I gown up from head to toe, which takes about ten minutes, before I go into his room.

"Who the fuck are you, faggot?"

"I'm your nurse." Aren't I the clever one with dialogue? Actually, I am kind of thrown for a loop. I never had a kid curse me out like this, and certainly no one ever called me a faggot to my face. I decide that I need to control the situation before he does.

"My name is Mr. Steele, I am your nurse. You are to address me as such. As for your comment on my sexuality I suggest that you do not know the first thing about gay people, or straight people, for that matter. I really don't care what your prejudices are—just keep them to yourself." I pause for dramatic effect. Somehow I feel like somebody's mother. "Now, I am here to start your dressing. First, I want to give you some pain medicine."

"What are you gonna give me and how much?" He appears jumpy.

Do I tell him? If he has been using drugs on the street he is going to need a lot more analgesic then what I can give him, and he knows it. Or is he just trying manipulate me into something else?

"What have you been using on the streets?"

"Nothin' man. Just a little pot."

"Good. Then what I'm going to give you will work like a charm. If you had done any heavy stuff then this wouldn't touch you."

I pick up the needle and show it to him.

"Wait a minute man . . ."

"My name is Mr. Steele."

"Hold on there, Mr. Steele." He is very nervous. He is pulling the covers up to his chest. "Karen, the other nurse, just gave me what I wanted and I didn't feel a thing."

I'm sure she did, I think.

He continues to fidget. "It's just like . . . gee, I don't know."

"What else have you been doing on the street outside of pot?"

I wait for an answer and after a moment he confesses. It appears that this kid has been into skin popping and snorting for some time. No one picked up on it because his burns destroyed all the usual tell-tale signs. It is going to be a long night. I leave his cubicle to figure out how much medication to give him before his dressing change.

I feel someone pinch my butt. I turn around and Harry is there. God, he is cute.

"What was that for?"

"I was testing your level of faggotness?"

"I can remember exactly were I was and what I was doing the moment I heard that Judy Garland had died, is that good enough?"

"Perfect," he says. "We're ordering in Chinese tonight. You want some?"

I fall in love with critical care nursing from the very first shift. The sheer challenge of it is more than I can handle. I never want to leave. This does not mean that my first night is not your average nursing horror show—it is. When I go back into my kid's cubicle with his pain medication he throws something at me.

"Catch! Mr. Steele!"

Instinctively, I grab it. It feels like a clump of barbecued chicken.

"What the hell is this?"

"My ear!"

He is very correct. I try not to puke.

I never actually leave the ICU and return to peds.

Six months pass and I am a full-fledged ICU nurse. I smoke nonstop and am only sober when I sleep and work. My diet has progressed to greasy diner food after work with Harry before hitting the bars. Harry and I become good and fast friends. He is the only person who can keep up with my drinking. Even Carmella is impressed.

It is 3 a.m. on a Tuesday morning. Harry and I are sitting in a new gay bar called the Pit Stop. The place is relatively empty. Only the desperate remain.

"I understand that Helen Hayes lives in Nyack," says Harry between sips of vodka.

"Well, I'm sure she'll be strolling in any minute. She is probably out in the parking lot having car sex."

Harry ignores my remark. A man of taste.

"Do you think we should?"

"Should what?"

"Have sex."

"Of course I do. What the hell do you think we're here for?"

A seven-foot-tall black man passes out at the end of the bar.

"Not a good sign," I say looking at our fallen brother.

"No, asshole. I mean with each other."

I had never really thought about it until that very moment. Sex with Harry. Sex with someone good-looking, intelligent, and nice. Sex with a good friend. Sex with someone I work with. Sex with someone that I would see almost every day. Forget it.

"Sex is easy. Friends are hard. Let's stay friends."

Harry smiles. "Agreed."

We leave the bar and head home in the mist of the night. Very Donna Reed.

"This is Brick. I'm down in the fuckin' emergency room with a stupid son of a bitch who tried to kill himself by jumping out a third-floor window. Some asshole, huh? No shithead ever bought it from the third floor." Brick yells back at the patient. "Gotta go higher asshole!"

I roll my eyes and begin to recite Hail Mary's. I am listening to the average bedside conversation of Dr. Brick Shine, trauma surgeon. I once asked him if Brick Shine was his real name. I mean how could it be?

"Go fuck yourself, queer boy!" the doctor replied.

"I can and do so frequently."

"Great. Wanna do some coke?"

My mind drifts back to what he is telling me about the jumper.

"So Steele, you fuckin' there man?"

"Yes, doctor."

"Hey you're okay for a faggot."

Acceptance. I am in heaven.

"What the patient's name?"

"How the living fuck should I know?!"

I can hear him snort.

"Are you doing coke?" I ask.

"No man. Just snot."

"Name?"

I can hear him turn his head away from the phone.

"Hey lady what's this Bozo's name?"

I can hear muffled sobbing in the background. He tells me the patient's name and that he will be up in the unit in ten minutes. I brace myself for the winds of terror.

Brick Shine is a short man with the same amount of class. He always wears clashing colors, which disturbs my sense of fashion, and he always has on mirrored sun glasses. I can see bits of his personality floating above him waiting to fall. He is by no means a real person. He is a cokehead with a license to practice medicine. His nose is constantly red from all the snorting.

The doors to the ICU crash open with Brick barging in with his hands held up in the air.

"I'm fucking here!"

The janitor washes his clogs with some dirty mop water. I look over at him and decide that it is time to move on. I can no longer take this bullshit. I decide that I will go nurse somewhere else. Somewhere without lunacy.

New York City.

But, before I can pack my bags I have to admit the new trauma patient and deal with Dr. Shine.

I quickly look at the patient that Brick has brought in. He seems stable. A broken shoulder is all. But you never know with jumpers. Within the first twenty-four hours after the jump they can develop all sorts of complicatons that need careful observation. I grab for the name on the identification band. Harrison Johnson.

"My name is Steele, Mr. Johnson. I'll be the nurse taking care of you for awhile. You're in the intensive care unit and it is about two in the morning." I say as I bend over the stretcher.

"Hey, Harrison, asshole. What is this—your third jump or what?" Shine yells while rubbing his nose. "You know man, next time go higher. I'm fucking tired of patching you up."

I do a quick assessment of the patient to get a baseline on his condition and hook him up to the monitors. Everything seems stable. No pain when I palpate his abdomen. Lungs clear. No vomiting.

Brick leaves, presumably to do some coke. Calm returns to the unit.

I gather up all the usual papers and start the admission paperwork. There is nothing more terrifying to an ICU nurse than paperwork. It appears to cloud the issue. I stick a cigarette in my mouth and a cup of coffee in my hand and head for the desk. I begin to wonder if anyone actually reads the stuff I am about to write. Maybe I should slip in some erotic poetry in the gastrointestinal assessment? I look across the room at the new admits monitor. His heart rate has slowed to fifty beats per minute. I get up and rush to his side.

His color has changed to putty. I cannot see his chest moving. Quickly I feel for a carotid pulse, and am unable to get one. Shit.

"I have a code situation here!" I say loudly. Within seconds every nurse in the unit is at the bedside. CPR is started. I am doing compressions. Another nurse is pushing drugs. Harry is doing mouth to mouth.

"Attention. Attention. Attention. Code Blue. ICU. Code Blue. ICU." I can hear the operator over the PA system intone without great passion.

"What the hell happened? He was fine not more than two minutes ago," says Harry.

"I don't know. I just noticed that he became bradycardic and when I got to the bed he wasn't breathing. I couldn't feel a pulse either."

One-one thousandanth. Two-one thousandanth. Three-one thousandth . . .

"EMD," says Harry, "This guy has fluid around his heart that won't let it pump. Where the hell is Brick? We have to tap this guy's heart."

By now the ICU is filled with dozens of people attempting to help with the code. Most are just getting in the way. No, that is not true. All of them are getting in the way. We do not need any more doctors to shout medication orders at us. Everything's been done. I still find it amazing that physicians actually believe what they order gets done and what they don't, doesn't. Ah, children at play.

My arms grow tired from all the chest compressions. I call for someone to take over.

"Were the fuck is Brick?" I shout. Cardiac and trauma surgeons are the only ones allowed to tap a heart. The other docs won't touch it.

Mr. Johnson's condition is critical. There is nothing more that can be done without evacuating the fluid around his heart. I decide to go find Brick.

I head immediately to the chief of surgery office. This is one of Brick's favorite hangouts to do a little coke at night.

I find Brick sitting at the chief's desk snorting coke off of his framed medical degree.

"What the fuck are you doing?"

"No mirror around, queer boy."

Brick bends over the diploma to snort his last line. I walk up to the desk and slam his head into the framed glass. It shatters and his forehead is cut. There is blood everywhere, including the chief-of-surgery sheepskin from Yale.

Brick just stares right at me with a rolled dollar bill hanging out of his nose.

"Listen fucker, Johnson just coded. EMD. He needs his heart tapped. I know that you are stoned, but you usually are. So get off that fat butt of yours and haul it into the unit."

"Yessir, your royal cocktease!"

With that he flies out of the office and down the hall with splatters of blood flinging in the background. I figure that his coke is really kicking in. I run after him. In the hallway back to the ICU I stop for just a few seconds and clearly think: "Why in the world am I a nurse? I could become a flight attendant and see exotic places."

Thoughts on career changing disappear as I hear Brick shouting in the unit. I rush back.

Brick is standing at the bedside with his mirrored sunglasses somewhat askew from his unfortunate accident with dried blood caking down his forehead. He is hyperventilating and rambling. I put one hand on his right shoulder and give him a firm squeeze.

"Dr. Shine will take an intracardiac needle and 50cc syringe," I say.

Harry hands him the needle and syringe.

"Do the tap now Brick, or I am going to bust your arm." I whisper into his ear. He nods and does the tap without any major problems.

Mr. Johnson's condition improves dramatically. The excitement is over. Everyone leaves, except the unit nurses. We assess and place Mr. Johnson on the right dosages of medicated infusions, and hook him up to a respirator. We will keep him under constant observation for the next twelve to twenty-four hours. One of us will be at his bedside at all times. Harry volunteers to stay with the patient for awhile so I can catch up on my paperwork and talk with Brick.

Brick is sitting in the storeroom on a box of IV solutions. He is trying to pull glass splinters out of his head. He looks up at me.

"What the fuck did you do that for queer boy?"

"Do what?"

"Bust my fuckin' forehead open, you dumb shit!"

"I don't know, it just felt right," I say as I shrug my shoulders.

Blood is all over his face,

"Here. Sign this," I say as I shove a piece of paper in front of him. "Just some orders that need an MD's signature." I lie.

"You know, you are fucking something else!"

"I know, and I thank God for it daily."

I fold the piece of paper in two and slip it into my pocket. Dr. Shine has just signed a note begging forgiveness from the chair of surgery for smashing his Yale diploma with a promise of a full explanation in the morning.

I take the signed paper and walk back into the unit to see how my patient is doing. Harry is at Mr. Johnson's bedside adjusting some medication to keep his blood pressure normal.

"You know Harry, I seriously question my choice of career at times like these. I could have been anything, a waiter, a florist, a hairdresser even, but no. I go into nursing."

Harry increases the amount of blood pressure medicine being given, and shrugs. "Some days chicken, some days feathers."

Harry, Carmella, and I are sitting at the bar in the Glory Hole. The crowd is thin even for a Thursday night. Just your average suit-and-tie closet cases who swear that nobody knows that they're gay, but, of course, no one is fooled. Not even their mothers. You cannot reach the age of forty-two without a girlfriend without some questions being raised. You know that they know when the questions stop. Even mothers don't want to know everything that their sons are doing.

"I think it's time for me to go nurse mankind elsewhere."

"That's humankind, you fascist slut." Carmella responds swirling her beverage to form thick tornadoes of liquor.

"I'm tired of it all." I lament. "I am tired of not being six four and hung to my knees."

"I never get tired of it," Harry says.

Great. Now I am providing straight lines for queers.

"I need something new. I need to go somewhere new. I need to see if I really am any good at nursing. I've been at the same hospital too long—four years when you count my training. I need to spring forth."

Carmella jams another cigarette into her mouth.

Bernie comes over to us with his standard tired look of someone who has seen it all and is unimpressed.

"That gentleman over there would like to buy you a drink." Bernie nods his head to the left to reveal a very nice-looking IBM executive type replete with standard-issue gray flannel suit.

"Well Harry, aren't you going to go over there and throw your beautiful self at him?" I say.

"It's *you* that he wants to buy the drink for Steele."

"Me?"

Bernie nods in tired amazment.

"Normal people don't buy me drinks. There must be some mistake." By now Carmella has turned and is directly staring at the guy in utter disbelief. Harry beings to giggle.

I look at my two friends. "Bernie, please tell that gentleman that I can only drink in threes." I say pointing at Harry and Carmella. "Tell him it is a religious thing."

Bernie nods once more and goes to deliver the message. A few minutes latter he returns with three drinks on his tray.

"I suppose this means that you all owe him a blow job now." Bernie says as he places the drinks in front of us.

"So which one of you queers is going to go over there and protect my good name. I don't do blow jobs for drinks." Carmella mutters as she downs the dregs of her last cocktail.

"Like I do!" I shout.

Both Harry and Carmella turn and look at me.

"Okay, so I do. Shoot me. It's not like it is illegal or anything."

"Well actually it is," says Harry.

"What the hell do you mean that it is illegal? You mean that any asshole can carry a handgun, but oral sex can land you in the slammer? My God, how many blow-job fatalities have you ever seen? Has anyone ever come up to the two of you in the ER screaming for attention because he just gave a blow job? Nurse, nurse! Stop me before I go down again."

"Actually, only once," says Harry.

"Sure."

"No, honestly. It was a few years ago and I had to float down to the emergency room because everyone down there had the flu or something," Harry says as he sips on his fresh drink.

I looked at Carmella to see if she was buying any of this. She wasn't.

"I was down there at about two a.m. when this big black guy built like a brick shithouse comes crashing through the doors with a blanket tied around his waist. I thought I was going to come right then and there. He was beautiful. But I noticed that he had beads of sweat across his forehead and he was hyperventilating. So I pitch my lust, and get him onto a stretcher so I can do a quick assessment. This guy still hasn't said a word to me."

I take some of my newly arrived drink and shoot a smile at Mr. Gray Flannel Suit as I lift up my glass in salute. You have to humor these poor bastards.

"So, here it is two o'clock in the morning and I am all alone with this guy and he isn't talking. Just doing a lot of groaning and holding onto his crotch. I go for the blanket thinking that he was in a fight or something and got kicked in the groin. But much to my surprise when I pull away the blanket this huge black erection greets me."

"Bullshit," I say

"No, no. It's true," Harry says. "It appears that he and 'a friend'," Harry does the inevitable quote-unquote signal, "got a little drunk and decide to play with each other. And in the middle of their play someone had placed a shot glass on the tip of his penis, and it wouldn't come off. I tried everything before I had to wake up the on-call doc. Lubricant. Tongue blades. Pulling. You name it. But nothing worked and I could see the tip of his penis turning blue. I figured that somehow a vacuum had been created. So I had to wake up the doc."

"Who was on call?" I ask intrigued and hoping it wasn't Brick.

"Donna Harrison."

"The bitch of all time," I laugh snorting out some of my drink through my nose.

"Oh she was incredible. All she kept on doing was screaming at this poor guy. She was yelling at him asking him didn't he know that there was a shot glass on the end of his dick, and couldn't he just yank it off himself before his entire dick had to be cut off. I mean I thought the guy was going to pass out! After all, what the hell did she think he was there for? Show and tell?"

Mr. Gray Flannel Suit is beginning to feel left out. He starts to get up and weaves his way over to us. A drunk. God I hate drunks. I take the final swallow of my drink and signal Bernie for another round.

"Dr. Harrison is hysterical now. This is truly something beyond her experience as a straight white girl. You know how Harrison is. Always perfect in appearance and stupid in judgment. I don't think she ever saw a black weenie before. So I decided to do the one sensible thing I can think of doing. I call maintenance."

We all looked up at the same time to see Mr. Gray Flannel Suit standing near us. He is definitely better looking under indirect lighting and at a distance. He stretches out his arms and belts out.

"Oh Lady of Spain I adore you! Oh Lady of Spain I need you! Oh Lady of Spain I want . . ."

And he then falls dead drunk to the floor.

"Thanks for the drinks," says Carmella ever so politely as she blows out a stream of smoke.

Harry gives him the quick once-over without getting up from his chair. Bernie comes over and scoops up the fallen soldier with professional dispatch and places him in a corner. Sort of like a drunken throw pillow.

"So this maintenance guy comes up and I explain the situation to him. He comes back a few minutes later with a glass cutter. Harrison is still ranting and raving but doing nothing. The maintenance guy is cool and calm, like this is no big deal. You know, shot glasses on weenies are everyday happenings. He just goes over to the guy and does a few zips with his glass cutter and taps the glass and it falls in two. I am astounded. Even Harrison shut up. The black guy is so happy to have his penis back in his hand again he can barely speak. Before any of us could ask any questions the maintenance guy turns and says, "No big deal really. I am the circumcision tech for my synagogue."

Carmella and I burst out laughing. Carmella is laughing so hard she falls over backwards in her chair. I go over and help her up. The few remaining customers are giving us dirty looks. How the hell are they suppose to pick up anybody with all the laughing going on in the corner?

"So what happened to the guy?" I ask.

"We dated for three months," says Harry.

"Now wait a minute," I say. "That is technically not a blow-job emergency. That was a penis problem. I don't think it qualifies."

Harry just shrugs his shoulders. Some days chicken. Some days feathers.

"Well, penis problem or not I still feel like I'm in a rut, and I want to try something new."

Carmella nods her head in the direction of Mr. Gray Flannel Suit now snoring loudly in the corner.

"I said new, not abused."

"So what are you going to do?" Harry asks.

"I think it is time for me to move to Manhattan. The bucolic lifestyle of Westchester is no place for a young gay man to be."

"It is if he wants to stay alive. New York is very dangerous," warns Carmella suddenly becoming very maternal. "Crazy people on every street corner just waiting to attack you. This I know. I read *Newsweek* regularly."

"Oh come on. It is the 1980s and everyone is hip. All that bullshit about New York is mythical."

The very next day I start calling all the major hospitals in Manhattan asking if they need any nurses. I am amazed by the response. Every single place I call tells me to name the day I want to start. There are jobs aplenty. You name it and it is there. ICU positions. ER positions. Anything. Also, the pay is nearly twenty-five percent more than what I am currently making. All the nurse recruiters are blabbing to me about their hospital and how wonderful it is.

By the end of the week I have an avalanche of brochures and letters. I cannot believe that anyone is all that interested in me. I am not all that interested in me.

As I sift through all the mail I decide that I am going to make a mature intelligent decision about my career. I'll find out what is the best gay bar in all of Manhattan and apply to those hospitals within a ten minute walk of its front door. Nurses can prioritize with the best of them.

Harry, of course, knows the bar of my dreams. Auntie Em's. It appears that Harry has spent many a night in Auntie Em's and swears that it is the only bar worth going to during the week. I ask about the weekends.

"Listen honey, I don't remember the weekends. At least not the good ones."

My walkable choices of hospitals are Bellevue and City Hospital. At Bellevue the recruiter asks me how much life insurance I have. This is not a good sign in my book. Naturally, I declined any further discussion. I do not want to fall into statistical prediction for Carmella.

City Hospital wasn't much better. The recruiter turns out to be a six-foot-four former Texan named Daisy McQueen. Daisy is a real charmer. She dresses in ridiculously frilly outfits with high collars that make her look like the loser in battle with a box of Kleenex. Also, she never smiles.

"I don't like to," she tells me. "And I don't have to. Probably something to do with my stupid name. Do I look like a Daisy McQueen?"

Indeed not, but then again, what does one look like?

Daisy sits ramrod straight as if she is about to explode.

"How do you feel about safety Mr. Steele?" Daisy doesn't talk actually, she clips.

Safety? Trick question I'm sure. I keep my mouth shut.

"Safety, Mr. Steele, is not real big around here. Oh, now don't get me wrong. We are as big as hell on it—talking wise. I can show you mounds of policies and procedures. It is all documented like crazy. Reality is another concept. We in the nursing administration don't deal with reality very well. Why should we? We're management. Strictly nine to five."

I swallow hard. My mind drifts back to my psych rotation in school. I wonder if she is having some sort of loosening of her ego boundaries. I also decide that I like her. I make a mental note to myself to think about going into therapy.

"I, however, am the renegade of the department. You see I actually go and do bedside nursing every now and then. Keeps me honest. The others think I'm Froot Loops. And they may be right. But the reality is the nurse-patient ratio here stinks. You could have up to four ventilated patients in the medical ICU. Sometimes CCU only has two nurses for the whole unit. You are not assigned any one unit. You float between all four units, MICU, CCU, SICU, and the Open Heart Unit. You go where the need is and do what you can. So what do you think?"

"Some days chicken. Some days feathers."

"Exactly. You're hired."

I am too scared to say no.

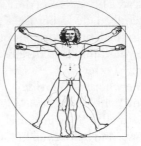

PART THREE

So I am off to the big city. I fully expect a tearful farewell from Carmella and Harry. My expectations die hard. They come with me.

City Hospital has a wonderful recruitment gimmick. Low-cost housing right in Manhattan. I am one of the lucky ones. I actually am able to rent a studio apartment with a sleeping alcove facing the East River. Not being a native city boy I don't have the faintest idea on why a sleeping alcove is such a big deal. I am informed by the housing office that not many people who live in Manhattan actually have a bedroom. Most people just sleep on their couches. I store this information for future use. I will make all the right oohs and aahs when a trick actually has a bedroom for us to frolic in.

Both Carmella and Harry come with me to see my new apartment. The woman in the housing office told me that I had to let her know if I want the place within the next two hours. After all she had a lot people on the waiting list. The only reason that I had even been offered an apartment was because I was an ICU nurse working the evening shift. I tell the housing lady that I will take the apartment sight unseen. She smiles apparently pleased with my idiotic decision. It makes her life easier. To hell with me.

The apartment is on Twenty-Eighth Street just off First Avenue and even has a doorman. Actually, he is a hospital security guard living up to stereotypical expectations. He is fat and asleep. We go up to the fifteenth floor without disturbing him. I feel safe and secure.

Carmella swings open the door to the apartment. We walk in but do not get very far. Immediately to our right is the bathroom. It is painted fire engine red. On the ceiling are hundreds of old wine bottle labels. The kitchen is the size of a car's back seat. The walls and the ceiling are a deep high-gloss purple. Someone has tastefully nailed a border of plastic grape vines around the top. I refuse to go into the living room out of shear fear.

"Who in the world do you think lived here before?" asks Harry.

"The whore of Babylon," I offer.

"I thought you were the whore of Babylon."

"No I am the yutz from Yonkers for having just rented this place."

"Oh come on," says Carmella. "It won't be that bad. Just a little paint. Couple of nice throw pillows, and before you know it—home. Let's see what awaits around the corner."

I grimace and lead the way. The living room is a big square room in pristine condition. Its walls are white and unblemished. The hardwood floor is in pretty good shape. The coveted alcove is a largish indenture in the far wall and is framed by an arch. It looks big enough for a twin bed and a few fantasies.

This is the apartment of my dreams if I can somehow avoid use of either the kitchen or bathroom. The living room windows look out over First Avenue, and if I stand on my tiptoes with my neck cranked 180° and squint I think I can see water. Or maybe it is New Jersey. Whatever. Both are safely out of my reach.

Standing in the middle of my new apartment I realize that this is my first real adult decision outside of my daily life-saving shtick. I am even beginning to think like a real New Yorker.

Carmella and Harry are discussing the various needs of my new abode when the doorbell rings.

"I'll get it!" yells Carmella. "I bet it is the Beaver. Probably forgot his poppers for show and tell."

One of the most remarkable things about Carmella is that for her enormous bulk she is extremely graceful. She can glide in and out of tight corners like a ballerina.

Standing in the doorway is the smallest nurse I have ever seen. She is on the critical downside of five feet. Her hair has been bleached to the color and consistency of straw. Her skin is creamy white. I know she is a nurse because she is wearing a T-shirt that reads: "I am a nurse so fuck off."

"Nice shirt," comments Carmella as she lets in my first visitor.

"Just a little something I had made up to promote the profession," she drawls through one of the heaviest Southern accents I have ever heard.

"Which one of you sugar babies is the new tenant?"

I raise my hand.

She gives me the once-over without any shame. "Oh honey," she cries. "If I weren't a born-again lesbian I could go for you. I bet you look mighty dandy in a pair of handcuffs." She stops and giggles. "Oh where are my manners!" She says as she extends her hand.

"I am Judi Katz. Can you stand it!" Judi is practically cackling at this point. "A Jewish Southern lesbian living among you dirty turncoat Northerners. You are just going to love this apartment!" Judi attempts to flip her straw from one side to the other without any success. "I had such great hopes of finishing the living room before I left. I had envisioned it as a tropical rain forest and nightclub. Sort of like the Copacabana with a Carmen Miranda dirge being played in the background." Judi's arms are outstretched as she spins around in glee.

The world has been spared.

"So you're the one responsible for all of this," beams Carmella. Judi practically gushes assent. "Do you know how many wine labels are stuck to the bathroom ceiling?"

"Four hundred and eighty three! Every time I finished a bottle of wine I just soak them off and slam the suckers up there."

"How long did you live here?" I ask, cringing inwardly.

"Three fucking months!"

Judi gives us her grand tour of the apartment. We find out exactly how she was going to transform the "boring Yankee living room into something of splendor." She would be thrilled to help me if I want to proceed. I demure.

Judi has just resigned her position as senior staff nurse on evenings in the ICU to transfer to the psych floor, and is moving in with a new girlfriend. I am beginning to see a pattern in my life. The psych unit is a fifteen-bed locked floor basically catering to the very rich and the very bored. It appears, according to Judi, that these two attributes usually equal a cocaine addiction.

Judi chatters on and accompanies us back to the housing office where I take care of the remaining paperwork. We depart the closest of friends. Judi will be in the unit for my first week. She promises to show me everything.

I am beginning to think I'll need that.

As three crazed people in search of a cure, Carmella, Harry, and I spend a very long weekend moving me into my new place. I decide to leave the bathroom red out of deference to Judi and my pocketbook. I can only afford to buy paint for one room. I will not live with a purple kitchen. The best that happens after five coats of white is that the walls are toned down to a pale grape.

It is the Sunday night before I start my new job. Carmella and Harry have decided to stay the night again and give me a grand send-off.

We spend the night looking out the window at the city as if it were some big beautiful wild animal held in captivity. No one even mentions going out. The rest of the evening is filled with getting stoned on some very good pot that Harry brought along and a lot of and giggling.

Hospital orientation doesn't begin until the rational hour of nine the next morning. Carmella and Harry head back to Westchester and we make plans for the coming weekend. I suddenly feel like crying.

"Don't," says Harry. "Your mascara will run and you will look like one of the nine thousand pictures of Judy Garland in despair."

Right as usual.

Hospital orientation is a total waste of time. We sit in a large room with all the other new employees while some low-level jerk tries to explain policies, procedures, benefits, and the meaning of bad karma in eight painful hours. I spend the time looking like I am paying attention but am having sexual fantasies. I start to develop pornographic story outlines in my head that I plan to sell to several gay magazines. Idle hands and pornography are a perfect combination. I decide my porn pen name will be Dik Sizemore.

I am the only man in the entire orientation. I feel awkward. At the morning coffee break I try to stand around and become invisible. I do not succeed. I foolishly attempt to get very involved in getting my cup of coffee hoping that it will kill the entire fifteen-minute break. It doesn't.

"Can I help you get your cup of coffee?"

I turn and see the all-American girl in living color. She has perfect skin and all the other mom and apple-pie-standard features. She also has nice tits. I remind myself that I am not a tit man. In fact, I suddenly feel very ashamed for even noticing her tits in the first place. I am probably just acting out some suppressed male dominance left over from the Stone Age. I decide that I need to work on my feminism. However, she still does have nice tits.

"Oh no thank you," I cleverly say. "I'm sorry I've taken so long." I try to smile and move along.

But the tits follow me.

"Married?"

"No."

"Girlfriend?"

"No."

"Gay?"

"Yes."

"Oh well. You just lost out on the blow job of a lifetime."

"And if I had wheels I'd be a truck." It was the only logical thing I could think of to say. I am beginning to wonder if everyone is so open about sex in New York. It seems to me to be a very casual thing. Almost like going out to lunch.

I survive general orientation. Barely. The next day we are to report to our respective clinical units at 7 a.m. for the first of four days of staff orientation. After that I will go onto the evening shift. I am excited. I will work from three in the afternoon to eleven at night. I cannot believe that anyone would want to work any other shift. I will have the whole morning to sleep in and the entire night to play.

I decided to reward myself with a few early-evening cocktails at Auntie Em's. I rush back to my apartment after orientation and take a quick shower. I am feeling very happy. Gay, even. In the shower I take stock of myself. I like what I see in the body department. I am muscular without being obscene, my skin is clear, and I decide that my face would not send anyone into spasm. Harry keeps telling me I need to work on my hair. I suppose that he is right, but who the hell wants hair that needs work? I think I need to become more fashion conscious.

But for now I am stuck with what I have. I dry off and change into jeans and a white button-down oxford. I slip on a pair of battered penny loafers without any socks. I reach for a splash of cologne and realize that I haven't had a bottle of cologne in my possession since nursing school. I mentally put it on my self-improvement list. In the meantime I just dab a bit of lemon extract on my neck. What the hell, maybe they will think I am a baker.

I stick a cigarette in my mouth and check my watch. 5:30 p.m. The after-work crowd will be there. Nice young executives having a martini before going back to their apartments or wives.

I make it to Auntie Em's before 5:45. It is divided into three sections. When you walk in the door there is a long bar with stools facing a wall with a drink ledge. At either end of the wall are two openings leading to a small room with a pool table and some benches, and a larger room where the disc jockey is encased in a Plexiglas booth.

I don't know what I was really expecting for the early evening crowd. Perhaps people just sitting around having a civilized drink and conversation. A little mood music perhaps.

The mood is frantic even at this early hour, and the music is Ethel Merman screeching "I've Got Rhythm" at the top of her sizable lungs to a crazed disco beat. In fact, she sounds like she is running away from a crazy man chasing her with an ax, uphill. I keep wondering if this record is Miss Merman's great joke on the world. I also wonder if maybe she fell and hit her head on something on the way to the recording studio and was forced into doing this by a crazed disco queen. (They should post a warning notice on the outside of any bar playing the *Ethel Merman Disco Album* as a last-ditch warning to those of us sometimes faint of heart.)

I decide to sit at the bar and attempt to have a quiet drink by myself. The bartender comes over to slam a clean paper napkin in front of me as the standard gesture of good will.

"You look like fresh meat."

"Would that be sirloin or chuck?"

"Neither. Name's Bernie," he says as he sticks out his hand.

Another bartender. Another Bernie. Maybe it is a union rule.

I order my Dewar's on the rocks and sit back. No one seems real interested in starting up any conversations. Everyone is too busy posing.

I sip on my first drink and take another long look around. I figure no one is going to move or say anything until at least eight o'clock. Not wanting to appear idle I ask Bernie for a pen and grab a few cocktail napkins. Ethel Mermen is finally quieting down in the background while some real disco diva belts out a tune. I write on top of one of the napkins:

THINGS TO IMPROVE MY LIFE

1. Think about stopping smoking.
2. Drink only Scotch.
3. Stop staring at tits.
4. Start exercising.
5. Refuse to learn any disco lyrics.
6. Know first and *last* names of the people I sleep with.
7. Know one interesting fact about them.
8. Date without sex. (The first night anyway.)
9. Come out to my mother.
10. Get serious about my career.

I signal Bernie for a refill. I look at my list and am impressed. This will become my personal ten-point plan for life enrichment. As I polish off my second drink I realize that I am already fulfilling my goals. Only Scotch has passed through my lips all evening. Being resolute isn't so hard I reason as I stick another cigarette in my mouth.

My first night out in the big city turns to bust and I walk home without smoking. If I can get home and go directly to bed without another cigarette then that will make me smoke free for about six-and-a-half hours. I am already gloating and thinking about my first cigarette in the morning with my coffee.

"You must be Steele." A tall thin black nurse says to me as I enter the ICU in the morning. "Judi had told me all about you. I'm Gloria," she says as she sticks out her hand to be shaken.

"Hi," I say. I must work on my socialization skills.

Gloria stands in front of me looking me up and down shaking her head.

"Judi was right. You are handsome for a white boy."

Before I need to respond and mark myself an all out asshole Judi comes sailing out the double doors to the unit.

"Oh honey, thank God you are finally here!"

Judi grabs me with both hands and hugs me hard.

Life in New York is good. I am finally feeling pulled together although I have not yet accomplished all my cocktail-napkin goals. Still, I am working and learning and loving my job, and I am out after work nearly every night of the week.

I do not develop any new sense of maturity but I have this incredible sense of urgency. Everything must be done right away. Probably from working in an intensive care unit. Every little move and action is urgent and vital. Sometimes it takes me up to two Scotches at Auntie Em's before I begin to function near the speed limit.

My newest urge is confirming my mother's worst fears. Her son is light in his loafers. Now I know that my mother already knows I am gay because I have told her since age eleven that I wanted to run away from home and marry Sky King. Sans his niece Penny. Let the little bitch go off and live with another relative. Perhaps a spinster aunt from St. Louis. That should do her in and then I can have Sky King all to myself. I would even overcome my nasty little habit of habitual air sickness for Sky. No vomit bag for me. Love is, if you pardon the term, in the air.

Now my mother never quite took to my Sky King outbreaks very well. I must say that is partly my fault. I always seemed to possess the best possible ability for selecting the worst possible moment. A trait, I am afraid, that I haven't outgrown. In fact, I have perfected it to a new level.

I announced my honorable intentions toward Sky King on one lovely Tuesday afternoon in front of Monsignor Boyd who had come to pay my mother a visit regarding my readiness to join the altar boys. If my memory serves me correctly my mother was bending over with a tray of tea sandwiches to the Monsignor as I proclaimed my desires and all action stopped. My first thought was that my mother farted and was going to die of embarrassment in mid-sandwich serve. I attempted to come to her rescue by announcing that I certainly didn't smell anything funny. By all means nothing like a fart or anything.

The priest was out the door before I could be saved by the Holy Spirit, and I was spared from the altar boys. I suppose being kicked off altar boys prior to serving is a rare and dignified accomplishment of any eleven-year-old.

My mother never spoke of Sky King again.

I made frequent Sky King moans and groans all to no avail. My desires were completely ignored. I even announced that I would not be going to my senior prom because Sky King wasn't available. The only reaction from my other was this:

"You checked?"

"Yup."

She blessed herself and continued to fold laundry. A real job for a real woman.

So letting my mother know that I was gay was just a matter of a formality. Like sending out wedding invitations. The thought of a smart-looking printed announcement had even crossed my mind. But when I went to Tiffany's and got a gander of the price of the paper I wanted I figured—fuck it. If someone was that close to me and didn't know I was gay, then they weren't that close to me.

I plot out telling my mother with Bernie the bartender. I have grown to like all the Bernies in my life and find that their advice is invaluable. A good bartender, like a good nurse, knows certain things that just cannot be learned in school.

I also ask Harry, Carmella, Judi, and Gloria for their advice. Not that any of their suggestions weren't good, but I distinctly felt that I was better off with my bartender. Both Harry and Judi suggested that I show up in drag as a modern-day Florence Nightingale.

"You want me to wear white at lunch!" I scream.

Judi suggests telling her that I was brainwashed by a bunch of Southern lesbians who threatened the free world if I didn't convert.

Since I don't give a damn about the free world I pass on this notion.

Carmella and Gloria, my beacons, suggest the "truth."

A strange and inviting concept that I readily agree with. After all, my mother and I already have the Sky King thing between us, and I am sure she already knows.

I have to ply my mother with guilt to come to the city and meet me for lunch. After all, she would have to take a twenty-minute train ride from the outskirts of Parkchester to meet me. She tells me she doesn't like the city. I tell her that she is technically a resident of the city living in Parkchester, which is in the Bronx after all. Oh, no she says, it is more and more like Westchester everyday. Never, I reply. Maps don't lie.

Having won the geographical argument with my mother I now have to select a meeting place. I decided on the Village. Coming out in Greenwich Village seems rather redundant, but I am hoping that by exposing her to healthy gay men and women she will not have a hissy fit.

We meet at the Bay Street Cafe located on Greenwich Avenue. It is a beautiful summer afternoon in late June. The air is perfect. In another week Manhattan will be a ghost town on the weekends and those of us remaining will turn surly. But, today is perfect.

I arrive at the restaurant a half hour before my mother is due and she is waiting for me. I curse myself for stopping at Auntie Em's for a glass of wine. But when I look closely at my mother I am sorry that I didn't have a second.

"Ma, you're early."

"Of course, you think I can control how fast those guys drive those buses? Believe me I would if I could. There were several moments that I thought I would wet my pants. And wouldn't you know today I am wearing cotton and not my usual nylon."

"Some days chicken, some days feathers."

"I never understood this chicken and feathers thing of yours. What does it mean?"

"Oh, I don't know Ma. It is hard to explain. It is a saying that I picked up from Harry. It means sometimes things are good and sometimes things are bad."

"This I understand."

"Good. Let's get a table."

My mother is not a slave to fashion. Outside of her self-proclaimed cotton panties there isn't a single natural fiber touching her body. My mother's philosophy is simple. No one in their right mind would buy clothes that required chemicals to clean them. Anything my mother owns can be tossed in the washer with any available household soap. Nothing she owns runs. It barely moves.

I stare at her outfit and feel a real sense of warmth. I am glad that my mother doesn't have any taste. I would hate having to compete with her. My nerves at this point decide to get in the way of clear thinking. Our waiter approaches. He is Adonis. I can feel the beginnings of an erection even before he speaks. So here I am drooling in front of my mother over the waiter and getting a hard-on. At this point in my life I sincerely wish I had gone to church more often because clearly only divine intervention is going to get me out of this one.

"Good afternoon. My name is Clay. Can I bring you folks a drink before ordering?"

A drink. What a fabulous idea.

"White wine, please." I manage to say without sounding like a dizzy queen. Well, not at first anyway.

"Wine! You drink wine! I don't believe such a thing. That my baby would drink wine, and in front of his own mother." My mother has started one of her scenes. I know better than to try to do anything about it. You just kind of have to ride it out, like a hurricane. "He will have nothing of the kind. Please bring my boy a Pepsi."

"Diet," I assert.

"The same for me Clay." Our waiter is smiling and walks away to reveal the world's most wonderful tush.

I am just settling back in my chair easing into my dirty thoughts when my mother interrupts.

"So is this the fancy lunch where you try to slug down wine and tell me about Sky King again?"

I wish I could say something, but I don't. My eyes try to dance out of my head.

"So you're gay. Big deal. Your father and I had that figured out since you were about six years old. You are the only boy in the world who begged for a Ken doll." My mother picks up the menu. "The meatloaf looks filling."

"That's it?" I am more than merely puzzled here. This was just too easy.

"Why of course that's it. What in the world did you expect? Perhaps you should want me to go into hysterics and slash my wrist with dull restaurant cutlery?" She says.

"Sweetheart," my mother says as she leans over the table toward me, "it is no big deal. You're happy and healthy and that is all that matters. Your problem is that you don't give older people any credit. You think that because your poor mother is nearly sixty years old she is out of touch. I understand many things in this life. Things that you will never have the opportunity to even think about."

My mother readjusts herself in her chair as Clay appears with our Diet Pepsis.

"My son has just made the most outstanding statement to me Clay," my mother says to our waiter. She talks to strangers with an intimacy that is not shared with her own family. She puts down her menu.

"My boy just told me he was gay." Poor Clay clearly does not know what to do or say. His well-manicured waitperson expression is beginning to crumble. I am rather enjoying watching him suffer. Nothing like having a nurse around.

"So," my mother continues, "I'll have the meatloaf, and perhaps you two should date. I mean you both have been making goo-goo eyes at each other since we got here."

My mother reaches down and ravages her "purse." Actually, I don't think that it would qualify as carry-on luggage for most airlines. She retrieves a piece of paper and a pencil.

"Look, Clay, this is my boy's number." My mother frantically scribbles on a napkin. "He's a nurse and has a good job. No schmuck stuff for him. Give him a call."

"'Schmuck'? Ma, we're not even Jewish. Where did this schmuck thing come from?" I say quickly glancing over at the piece of paper checking it for accuracy.

"So, Clay, you have a phone?" My mother demands. I turn red.

"Sure," he monosyllables. "Here." He hands her his hastily scrawled number.

Clay leaves without taking my order. But he has my phone number which is, of course, more important.

I look at my mother in a whole new light. For the first time she appears to be a real person. I had never really thought of my mother as a person; more like a commodity. You know, all-purpose mother, right off the shelf.

"So, now that I know that you're gay do you somehow feel liberated?"

"Well, no actually. I feel . . ."

"You should feel ashamed." Alas, my real mother returns. Her mind was not sucked out by homosexual aliens as I had begun to suspect.

"Ashamed?"

"Ashamed! You should feel terrible for putting your poor mother through this. I mean for years I had to watch you watch all the other boys, and you never said anything. You are my boy and I decided long ago just to accept." My mother says in a staccato voice. "Fuck everyone else."

I stand up and frantically search for Clay. I am flailing my arms frantically. My mother babbles on and on.

"My mother just said 'fuck'! I want a drink! I want a Scotch!"

My initial impulse is to slap my mother across the face.

Clay comes scurrying over in restless excitement.

"She said what?!"

I suppose that Clay feels just like part of the family at this point. I cannot bear to repeat it. I mouth the "F" word.

"Please just bring me a Scotch on the rocks."

Right now I am in no mood to get chummy with a stranger. My mother doesn't care that I am gay and is going around cursing. I somehow feel that reality has taken an irreversible turn around the bend.

Clay returns with my drink and gives my mother a harsh, disapproving look. I nod consent in his direction. My mother continues to talk about everything that she usually talks about. Life in the Bronx. Life at Immaculate Blessed Virgin Church. "Now there was a woman!" my mother repeatedly said after any mention of the church.

I am allowing the Scotch to work its way into my brain. I am hearing only fragments of my mother's monologue.

"Your Aunt Cece always thought you were queer. Is 'queer' okay? I don't know. I suppose not . . ."

I look up over my mother's head and see a muscular Italian man standing on a rooftop of a brownstone across the street. I take another gulp of Scotch and my mind drifts between my mother and the man on top of the building.

"So I said to that new priest that just started that I didn't even want to hear anything about going back to Latin masses. Who the hell understood what was being said. I can barely understand a lot of it now in English. But he said . . ."

The man is totally naked.

"I've decided not to run as president next year of the Ava Maria Guild. I mean, I have been president for the past six years. Let someone else have the headaches. It is a very tough job . . ."

The man is masturbating.

"Doing the Christmas fair alone would kill a horse."

A naked man is standing on a rooftop masturbating on a bright sunny day in Manhattan while my mother speaks. My eyes are glued to the action behind my mother's head. I have also decided to stop breathing. I figure it is better for me to suffer brain death than to have my mother turn around.

I finish my Scotch. Enter my good old buddy Clay with the very filling meatloaf.

I pick up my glass and shake the ice cubes to signal for another drink. My mother's objections to any alcohol seemed to have faded with the use of profanity. My mother keeps on talking. Clay gives me profound disapproving looks. I nod for him to look in the direction over my mother's head. He quickly glances up and notices the action on the rooftop. He freezes and gasps for air.

"This one's on me," he says as he slowly backs away.

My mother continues her fragmented speech as we lunch on the meatloaf. I consider becoming a vegetarian. The man on the roof continues to play with himself. God, he has staying power. Thankfully, my mother never turns around to see the anonymous masturbator. But I watch for us both.

As Clay hands me the check we hear a muffled round of applause as the naked man climaxes. My mother takes a small but smart bow. I just want to get her the hell out of here.

I walk my mother to her bus stop and see that she gets on the right one back to the Bronx. We don't say much in the process. At the station I suddenly feel sad.

"Look, ma . . ."

"Shss." She puts her finger up to her lips. "Everything is okay. One of the things you learn in life as you get older is to accept. People who never learn that miss out on a lot."

Her bus comes and she steps inside becoming just another New Yorker.

I call Harry on the phone and tell him about my mother and the man masturbating.

"You're making this up!" he screams.

"I am not! I am not that talented."

A pause.

"So what did you do?"

"I had another drink."

"Very wise."

I am now working the evening shift and am beginning to feel like a nurse again. No more orientation. I see the waiter Clay just once. He lives in Queens. Any self-respecting New Yorker will tell you gay people do not live in Queens. The joke potential is just way too easy.

Also, his burning ambition in life is to become Liza Minnelli. Unfortunately, Clay is a muscular Nordic man and any attempt at transforming himself into a waiflike Italian would be just plain disastrous.

How will I break the news to my mother? I am certain she has started picking out the silver pattern.

The evening shift is an interesting transition. It starts out very high powered with report and rounds and everybody making sure they can find at least one mistake the day shift made. The sun sets and lights dim and we try to pretend that these people will be getting some rest. Rest is not a reality in an environment that is nothing except strange and horrifying. All ICUs are full of machines and smells. The funny thing about working in the ICU is that you stop noticing the smells, and the cadence of the respirators becomes soothing.

The group on evenings is young and happy. Frequently after work we will get together and go to Farmers on Second Avenue for a late dinner. Having dinner during working hours is something I had long forgotten was a basic right. The unit is too busy. We grab cookies or saltines and stuff our faces and slug down coffee.

Jill has just moved to Manhattan from Arizona. She is a big-boned woman with a smile larger than Carol Channing's. She is also the same nurse who questioned a young doctor's insulin order on a diabetic patient. She couldn't make out the guy's handwriting. Did he write 10 units or was it 100 units? A very sizable difference that could have seriously injured the patient. The doc couldn't make out his own handwriting and began to mumble. Jill grew impatient. This was his own fucking handwriting. It was his patient. Didn't he know what the patient should get?

The poor slob was flipping through his notes not getting anywhere when Jill blew up.

"Look sweetheart, take a guess! I'll tell you if it's right!"

She did this on her first day. Actually, it was her first morning of clinical orientation. I liked her immediately.

The evening shift is quiet tonight. I think about going home and calling Harry and Carmella. I want them to come spend some time with me in the city. Actually, I keep on thinking about the three of us getting an apartment together. Maybe I don't drink enough?

Jill announces she is fucking hungry and wants to go to Farmers. There are always takers. About ten of us go over after work.

The people at Farmers are used to us. When we walk in after midnight they reopen the kitchen and let us order. Usually, we are about the only ones there except for some leftover straight people not talking to each other.

The meals are typical. Burgers and fries. Maybe a spinach salad. A few white wines. We laugh and giggle and gossip. People begin to leave. I check my watch. It is only 1:30 a.m. The bars don't close until 4:00 a.m. I can run home and change and hit Auntie Em's.

I finish my white wine as Jill tells another story about how she lost her virginity.

"Your story keeps on changing. I've heard you say you lost your virginity at least seven different ways since you came to work here."

"Why of course," Jill snaps. "I haven't been here that long." Jill pauses and readjusts her breasts. "I love my tits," she says into her bosom.

I polish off another glass of wine.

"In fact I think I can lose my virginity again tonight if you would like." Jill says this to me as she unbuttons her blouse two buttons.

"Jill, I'm gay."

"Honey, I know that. I only go to bed with gay men."

I stare at her. She has got to be kidding.

"Gay men are a challenge. Anyone can get a straight man hard, but it takes a real woman to make a gay man erect."

"You're kidding."

"Best blow job you'll ever have," says Jill.

"I doubt it," I say. "I give the best blow job in the world."

Jill howls as she throws her head back.

"That is what is so nice about gay men—you can talk about cocks with them."

"And swallowing."

"Swallowing!"

Jill and I leave and head for home. She lives in the same hospital housing complex that I do. Jill puts her arm around me. We are both still sober.

"Jill," I say. "I really am a very happily confirmed homosexual. If I could take a pill that would make me straight I would, but I'd rather toss myself off the Empire State Building at high noon. I am sure you are wonderful in bed. I know that I am. I have references."

"That is okay Steele." She puts her arm around my shoulder. "I am tired of men—straight or gay. I need a rest."

We walk in a comfortable silence for a few minutes.

"Do you know what I think we should do tonight?"

"No."

"Go to the Crisco!" She says as she spins around.

"What is the Crisco?" I ask dumbly.

Jill stops dead in her tracks and looks at me. I look at her. She jumps out into the street and frantically waves down a taxi.

Jill pushes me into the cab.

"The Crisco please!"

"Sure lady."

So we are off to the Crisco at 2 a.m. in our white nurses' uniforms. Pray for me Clara Barton.

The Crisco Disco is somewhere in lower Manhattan. The cabby just knows where to take us and I don't pay any attention until Jill pulls me out of the taxi and onto a gutter of a street. I step over a gentleman who obviously does not hold his liquor well. Very charming at the 2 a.m. hour.

"We're a little early for anything interesting to really happen tonight." Jill announces as she checks her watch. "Follow me."

Jill walks right up to this dirty brown door without any lights or signs or anything. She knocks. A few seconds later the door opens.

"You're going to love this."

What I am going to love is being gently placed against a wall by the meanest looking man I have ever seen in my life and being frisked.

"Jill, what in the hell is going on here! What the fuck is this guy looking for?"

"Weapons."

I turn toward the man with his hands going over my body. "You're looking for weapons?"

He shrugs.

He then searches Jill who enjoys the encounter tremendously.

"You have taken me to a place that searches for weapons before letting us enter?"

"You bet. Not many of these places left."

"Go figure."

After the weapons search we are allowed to buy tickets for drinks—beer only. No money is allowed on anyone. All valuables are checked at the door. Less chance of turning clothing into weapons.

We finally enter the Crisco and I am awestruck.

I look around the room and decide that I lack ethnic diversity in my life and that I need to make more black friends. I will add this to my cocktail napkin list.

The crowd is light.

"No one really comes here 'til fourish," Jill informs me.

Beyond the four-sided square bar that sits in the middle of the floor is a twenty-five-foot can of Crisco. Music blares. Men and women in various states of undress are dancing frantically in front of it. Everyone at the bar seems bored, maybe they are waiting for the four o'clockers to show up.

So Jill and I stand and stare up at this enormous Crisco can and all I can think about is bringing Harry here. I feel like I have just been consumed into a sleazy cult. I love it.

It is hot as hell on the dance floor. Jill and I look like perennial virgins all dressed in white. Why in the hell do nurses where white uniforms when it is one of the dirtiest jobs in the world?

We dance. The music vibrates deeply in my bones. I stare at the bodies around me. The men are very muscular and I vow to get serious about my working out first thing in the morning. Jill unbuttons her blouse to her waist, and I do the same.

A black man with dyed blond hair wearing only a leather jock strap comes over and kisses me on the mouth and sticks a small bottle under my nose. Poppers. I have never done poppers before. The feeling is incredible. My head and heart race. I feel like coming twenty times. I feel like I can.

He turns to Jill and starts to massage her tits. She laughs. I laugh. The blond black man laughs. Life is good. I am fucked up.

I am hotter than hell, and I take off my shirt. I am muscular and solid. There is not an ounce of flab on me and I am very well-defined. I really need to go to the gym I remind myself. Genetics die at age forty.

I am not sure of time and place as the poppers and beer weave into my head. I am not even sure I know who I am dancing with since Jill comes up behind me and presses a cold beer into the small of my back. I turn around.

"I thought you could use this." Jill shouts above the music. I nod in appreciation and slug down half the beer. I am drenched in sweat.

"What time is it?" I shout back.

Jill looks at her watch. "Six."

I stop dead. "It is six o'clock in the fucking morning?!"

Jill laughs and dances away with some scary-looking babe in leather. I look at the large crowd of sweating bodies and begin to laugh to. After all, Jill and I have to be back at the hospital in less than nine hours and we were still drinking and dancing.

I am certain that Florence Nightingale had nights like this.

Jill and I leave around 7:30 a.m. We gather up all of our personal effects and head for the door.

"Now, be brave." Jill warns as she pushes open the door.

"God," I say. "It's daytime."

"I know. Isn't it weird? I always feel like Bette Davis recovering from some fatal illness whenever I leave this place."

I stand and stare out at all the daylight. People are going to work and school. Jill and I are just going home from a night out. I should definitely start going back to church.

"Come on sweet cakes we have to get some sleep before heading back to the land of equal-opportunity illness."

Life is hell once again. I am in the ICU and I am alone. So much for patient safety. Daisy McQueen was right. No one here really gives a shit about patient safety and nursing care. More attention is given to car assembly line workers. Fuck Detroit. Right now I am ass deep in the medical ICU with six respirators humming to various mucus levels. Peritoneal dialysis bags hang in two cubicles as the magic fluid pretends to flush out toxins.

I am alone except for a nurse's aide, Mrs. Day, whose entire mission in life is to make sure everyone gets a back rub. She approaches the art of rubbing backs with the fervor of a religious zealot. This is great except she cannot prioritize. She would give a back rub to a corpse. One day, as I was turning a patient on her side to allow her to vomit, along comes Mrs. Day to slap on her lotion of love. The patient began vomiting down my pant leg, which did not exactly make me bond with her, all the while Mrs. Day is cooing on the joys of a nice back rub. I was contemplating the joys of caked vomit in my groin. Not going to be a good night for a date.

So, I am alone except for Mrs. Day. Everyone is at a dinner. I am the charge nurse tonight so in order to accept that honor, which carries total responsibility but no additional money, I also get to forgo any dinner. I am a leader. I am showing I am strong. I am a fool. It is me and Mrs. Day and eight critically ill patients. All I am doing is going from bed to bed making sure everyone is staying alive until the gang returns. I don't give a rat's ass if everyone is comfortable, but I will not let anyone die. Call it professional pride but no one is going to die on me while I am alone.

I glance of the clock on the wall. It is nearly 8:30 in the evening. Where the fuck is everyone? Having another round without me? It is getting late. I have to start giving out some meds before the rest of the staff returns. I'll show them. I will do it all. They will be so embarrassed. I will be super nurse. They will have had supper and a smoke. Ha! I am a fool.

I walk into one of the cubicles and look at the poor bastard in the bed. If he only knew how badly his open-heart surgery would turn out I am certain he would be sitting on a beach in the Bahamas right now sucking down a rum drink waiting for the end. Instead, he is in four-point restraints with a feeding tube up his nose and tracheotomy attached to a ventilator. Oh well, some days chicken, some day feathers.

I look over the five different IV medications hanging from the ceiling and glance at his monitor. Drips are dripping the correct amount and his vital signs are stable. Great, not looking for trouble here. I pick up the tube of nitropaste to give him his evening dose of nitroglycerin. I carefully measure out the correct amount on a piece of paper and slap the 1.5 inches of medicine on his chest. I stand back and watch to see if his blood pressure remains stable. Nitropaste is a great way of giving nitroglycerin but it can really drop a patient's blood pressure if too much is applied or it is rapidly absorbed.

I look out the window and see Mrs. Day doing her thing oblivious to anyone or anything else. Someone could be puking up monkeys and she would just hum her hymns and do her back rubs. A woman on a mission is an incredible thing to witness. I walk into the next cubicle. Another poor bastard suffering the same unhappy outcome from open-heart surgery. I make a mental note to myself to take better care of my heart. This open-heart surgery thing just needs more time to become a real viable treatment.

I look down at this other man tied to the bedrails and think that restraining humans is cruel. Now, there is nothing wrong with consensual bondage between adults, but I doubt if this guy is getting off on it right now. What we (in the great community of healers) are trying to prevent is the patient ripping out all the tubes that take us hours to put in. We hate to have to repeat our work over and over again. After all, we are the professionals. They are just the patients. We know best dammit.

I do my med thing and glance at his vital signs. Another victory for stability. Still no returnees from dinner and I am getting pissed. They are taking advantage of my easygoing ways. I will nail their tits to their asses when they walk through the door.

Out of the corner of my eye I see Mrs. Day approach one of the beds against the wall. This is the place affectionately known at the "cabbage patch." These are the folks just waiting for the good Lord to call them home or a bed in a nursing home to open up. Whatever comes first is fine with me at this point. Typically the cabbage patch is assigned to one nurse on the evening shift. Just a matter of watering them really.

Mrs. Day is turning one of the female cabbages on her side and announces that the infamous back rub is about to begin. She turns the patient on her side and exposes her butt and backside. She does this with the flourish of real showman. *Ladies and gentlemen in the cabbage patch tonight Mrs. Day and her back rubs!!!*

I watch as Mrs. Day picks up some ointment for the rub. It takes me a full moment to realize what is about to happen before it does. Instead of the back lotion Mrs. Day has picked up a tube of nitropaste. Before I can make it out of the cubicle and stop her she squirts at least half of its contents into her hands and is beginning to rub them together. Mrs. Day goes from being a black woman to a chalk-white woman in a New York minute. Her eyes roll to the back of her head before she crashes to the floor. I run to Mrs. Day and yell for someone to call a code. Like who is listening?

When I get to her side Mrs. Day has stopped breathing and I cannot get a pulse. This is just fucking great. Now I am coding staff members. This is not good night in Gotham.

I am compressing Mrs. Day's chest when I hear something backfire. A car? Gunshots? I should be so lucky. No. The nice cabbage-patch lady Mrs. Day was about to minister to is farting her brains out. I can only pray that gas is all that is going to be passed.

I tilt Mrs. Day's head back to do mouth-to-mouth when a unit clerk walks by the door of the unit.

"Hey! What you doin' there with Mrs. Day queer boy?"

"Finding Jesus, asshole! Call a code!"

The befuddled clerk finally puts two and two together and runs for the phone. As I hear the code called I know that it will be just seconds before I am surrounded by more people than I want to be at any time in my life. Expect for at the baths.

Mrs. Day is beginning to pink up but still not responding. I cannot even imagine how much nitropaste is pushing her blood pressure down to her toes. As I switch from mouth-to-mouth to chest compressions the door slams open, and in streams the evening crew. All of them are wearing Mickey Mouse Happy Birthday hats and streamers. I am only mildly surprised by this.

"What the hell happened?" Someone asks from the crowd.

"Got bored and lonely," I yell back.

With that I explain about the nitropaste and the chain of events. One of docs begins to snicker.

"This is one for the books."

Yea, I think. The book of medical horrors. How to kill your staff without really trying. I try to think of a new career. The thought of being a flight attendant surfaces again. Serving cheap wine and bad food suddenly has an appeal that I cannot deny.

The desire to change vocation becomes stronger as I hear someone in the crowd give a small but meaningful gasp of disbelief.

And then comes the smell. The unmistakable odor of fecal matter. The cabbage-patch lady has decided to shit her brains out. Since timing is everything in life I can only assume my place in heaven has certainly been confirmed as I smell the poop, and know it is only a matter of seconds before it comes into contact with me. I figure this gives me carte blanche to be a devil since being crapped on while doing CPR on a co-worker has to be right up there with parting the Red Sea.

Suddenly no one is talking. No one is trying to take over for me. I continue to keep Mrs. Day alive and feel the distinct ooze of poop flow from the bed above onto my back. I try to ignore this. I am not very successful.

"Would someone mind making sure that the patient that is shitting on me is okay?"

The scene goes on for another fifteen minutes when Mrs. Day finally comes around and is admitted to the Coronary Care Unit. She will be observed for several days. I, however, will have to report back to work tomorrow night.

I am contemplating masturbating with nitropaste to see if there is any erotic effect.

Someone has tactfully covered my back with a blanket. After all the hub from the bub dies down I look around and see everyone looking after all the patients. In some strange way I feel good. They are still wearing their Mickey Mouse party stuff but working.

I run to the locker room and toss my crap-laden whites into the trash, and take a quick shower. I put on scrubs. I make a mental note to do something about the uniform policy.

When I return to the unit everything is calm. All the patients are bedded down, the lights are low, and the hum of the machines returns to its pleasing cadence. In the middle of the nursing desk is a big birthday cake with my name on it.

Did I forget my birthday? How old am I? This is pathetic.

The staff is standing around with their silly Mickey Mouse hats on and they begin to sing a new version of Mickey's theme song.

"M-R-S D-A-Y and C-P-R to boot! . . . MRS DAY . . . CPR . . . MRS . . . CPR . . . MRS DAY . . ." Because she needs forever compressing the sternum deep . . ."

"What the fuck is going on?!" I shout.

"Just a little tribute to our hero." I hear from deep in the group.

The voice is so familiar. I suddenly freeze. It is Myles.

I walk up to him. I am in no mood for him.

"May I ask what you are doing here?" I pause. "No. Let me back that up and ask how did you find me?" I pause again. "And why?"

Myles smiles at my sheepishly. "Thought you'd like to know I am now divorced and was hoping we could go out for a drink or something."

"Myles I don't think that would be wise. Last time we dated you went off and got married to a woman. These things kind of stay stuck in a guy's memory."

He puts his hands in his pockets and says, "I was a jerk."

"Yes you were."

"Don't I get another chance?'

I think for a moment. "Nope."

"Really?"

"Really," I confirm as I turn and cut my birthday cake.

"Oh well, it was worth a shot." So much for wanting me back. "Hey, Steele, can you at least tell me a good bar to go to so I can get laid tonight?"

Without even thinking twice I pull the waist of his pants toward me and shove a big piece of birthday cake down and squash it.

After a moment of stunned silence Myles walks away with frosting and cake falling out of his pants.

I feel wonderful.

I finally encounter Nurse Kitten Doyle. She is legendary and deranged. I have managed to avoid any contact with her since she usually works day shift. But this evening we come face to face.

She is beyond the valley of bizarre. Kitten truly hates nursing. She hates everything to do with nursing or patients. Kitten is also about as feline as a porcupine at a Baptist barbecue. She is harsh, abrasive, and rude. And those are her more charming features. She also dresses as a pristine nurse just to make fun of her entire cosmic situation. Kitten comes to the unit attired in starched nurse whites, school cap, and the once-traditional blue cape with red satin lining. She looks like she has just molested Cherry Ames.

Her mission is to mock nursing by her attire and attitude. She almost succeeds except for the unrelenting fact that she is totally unlikable. No one can stand her. Also, she is a rotten nurse, and a coke addict.

Kitten comes storming into the unit in her nurse drag obviously suffering from recent cocaine ingestion. White powder still clings to her upper lip and her cape. Her nostrils are almost as manic as she. They flare as she flares.

Slamming into report Kitten sits down like a large seaplane hitting the East River. "Well, I am fucking here!" she says as she massages the coke remains into her nose. I watch as the last little bit buzzes her and she hits a new high.

I am speechless as I watch Gloria stare her down.

"We are so fucking happy Kitten," Gloria says without any trace of warmth. "Now sit your white ass down and shut up."

Meat could hang from the ceiling in the room. No one is breathing except for Kitten trying to snort in the last remains of her coke.

Shift report goes as per usual. Kitten is not even a flash point after her dramatic entrance. She is just a nurse in drag taking up space.

I move in my seat uncomfortably as if to dodge the ice cubes being lobbed from the inner sanctums of everyone's mind. Finally, report ends and I get the hell out of there and go to my patients. I do not want anything to do with Kitten Doyle and her antics.

Both of my patients are in septic shock. Every conceivable tube is plugged into every conceivable orifice. Patient number one is stable and going to make it. Patient number two is sicker than Kitten Doyle's attitude. I give him only a twenty-five percent chance of seeing the light of day again. He keeps me hopping all evening.

Near the end of the shift I am adjusting his blood pressure infusion to make sure his brain stays functioning. For what I don't really know. The days of counting his toes to show higher functioning are over. As I ponder his fate I hear Gloria scream out.

"Holy fucking hell!" Gloria yells.

I run toward Gloria's voice. I cannot imagine what is going down but it must be major. No ICU nurse screams unless there is alcohol or a penis involved.

I rush into the cubicle where Gloria is standing bracing herself in the doorway. The color has drained from her face. Nurse Doyle is inside the room putting a toe tag on her patient. I quickly scan the monitor and see a slow but visible heartbeat and blood pressure. The man is still alive.

I also see Nurse Kitten has placed a shroud underneath his body. He is all set for the final wrap.

Gloria's eyes are popping out of her head.

"What the fuck is this Kitten?" Gloria says evenly.

"What the fuck do you mean?" snorts Kitten as she wipes her nose. "This guy is circling Cincinnati for a fast landing and I don't want to have to stay late bagging him for the deep freeze." Kitten is calm and continues to prepare the living for death.

I take a step back and look deep into Gloria's eyes. There is a mixture of pain and anger dancing wildly in her head.

Gloria is trying to remain calm and professional. She presses her hands to her hips in order not to put them around Kitten's neck. "We do not wrap and toe tag the living you dumb little shit."

Okay, so professionalism be damned.

"What the fuck is the big deal?" Kitten honks back. "He's buying it in about fifteen minutes and I wanna go home."

"Get out," I say. Kitten just stares at me. "Gloria, take Kitten out of here. I will take care of this."

Without another word Gloria leads Kitten Doyle off to the great beyond. I only hear the yelling. I never see Kitten again.

I gently take the death wrap off the patient and sit with him until he dies an hour later. I curse Kitten Doyle.

The next evening I walk into report five minutes late and Gloria gives me the evil eye. I decide not to say anything smart for fear of my life. I go and apologize to her when report finishes.

"I'm the one who's sorry, Steele," she says. "This has been just one fuck of a day. You are not going to believe what is going on inside the cubicle."

Gloria just shakes her head without any additional explanation and leaves. I look around the room and see disbelief on all the other nurses' faces.

"They're spitting on him?" Jill asks no one in particular.

"That's what she said."

"Who's spitting on who?"

"The guy in the second cubicle."

The guy turns out to be Jerome Valentine, the Broadway producer. From the chart it appears that Mr. Valentine fell down a pretty steep flight of concrete steps causing numerous internal injuries and fractures. He was drunk at the time and no one really knows how long he was injured before he was found. To literally add insult to injury, Mr. Valentine is seventy-eight years old. All things considered, the prospect of another opening night party for the old guy seems fairly remote.

The entrance to the now-infamous cubicle is taken up with a mink coat. I decide that people who wear mink rank right up there with baby killers. The mink coat appears to have a life of its own. It is moving up and down with its occupant's gestures and speech.

"You are the world's biggest fucker!" The mink coat hisses. "If this wasn't a hospital I would really let you have it, you goddamn piece of shit!"

I walk up behind the mink coat.

"That's it. Go easy on him," I say.

The mink coat turns around and I become speechless. It is my all-time favorite actress. Linda Harper. The infamous Linda Harper. The Linda Harper who has won every major award for her singing and acting. She is also the one who exposed her tits on the *The Tonight Show*. Thank God I watched that night. Johnny Carson's interview with her was going right down the tubes and Linda said so. Johnny gave his usual Midwest laugh and said that yes, this wasn't his greatest moment on the show. Linda laughed and said well maybe this was. And then she ripped open her blouse and let her tits fall out coast to coast. Of course her tits were censored, but that made it even more fun.

I manage to regain my control, which of course should tell you something right there. "Excuse me, Miss Harper, but you can't . . ."

"Can't what?!" She yells. "Look sonny boy. I can do anything I want to. You should pardon the expression but I don't fuck with no low-life orderly."

"I'm no orderly!" I shout back.

"Then who the fuck are you?" she says staring at my white uniform. "The fucking Good Humor man?!"

I will remain professional.

"I am the fucking nurse." That's right Steele, go for the gold. "And this is my fucking patient, and you are a fucking moron."

"Moron? You calling me a moron?"

"Actually, a fucking moron to be exact."

"I could have your job for speaking to me that way."

"I doubt it even for a second." I say back and believe it.

"You're just a fucking nurse."

"Wrong. You're just a fucking actress. Nursing is vital and important to how people literally live and die. There aren't enough people in the world who are willing and smart enough to be a nurse. Don't get me wrong. What you do is important also. However, there are thousands of people willing and able to take your place. It looks like you lose out to the old supply and demand ratio." I cross my arms for dramatic effect.

"Nice speech," Linda Harper smiles. "Have you had the occasion to use it much?"

"Second time. Warren Beatty was number one."

She throws back her head and laughs. "You're making that up."

I shrug. "Some days chicken, some days feathers."

She turns back to Jerome Valentine. "You are lucky he's here, because if he wasn't I would disconnect your respirator and stick the tubes up your tired old asshole."

"I really think you should leave. Mr. Valentine needs care and I think you could use a drink."

"Would you join me?"

I just look at her like I am waiting for a bus.

Her eyes widen. "Would you join me for a drink?"

"I'm on duty."

"I meant when you get off."

"It's late. After elevenish."

"That's okay. I cleared it with my mom."

"I'm sorry, I didn't mean . . ."

"Yes or no?"

"Yes." What the hell?

"Good. I'll pick you up in front of the hospital at quarter past."

Before I can even nod she turns toward the patient and spits on him.

"He's a real fucker," she says to me as she leaves.

Caring for Mr. Valentine during the shift is a real challenge. I am nearly jumping out of my skin over the prospect of having a drink with Linda Harper. I am depressed because I know she is not going to show. I am frustrated because the patient tries to die every other hour. No one is going to die on me after being spat upon. No way is that going to be someone's parting memory of this world.

Mr. Valentine develops a tension pneumothorax a few hours after Linda Harper leaves. His vital signs become unstable and I can hear breath sounds over only one lung. I call for a chest X-ray and page the doctor covering the unit. By the time she is there the film is hanging on the view box displaying a very clear picture of a collapsed lung.

Mary Butler, MD, is the biggest and blackest woman I know. We have a great deal in common. We both know what it is like to be a minority in a gender-opposite profession. She is a black woman dealing with male physicians. I am gay and dealing with female nurses. It is not easy. Both of us know this and we are kindred spirits deep down.

In fact, it was Mary Butler who altered the "Doctors Only" sign in the cafeteria that roped off a section for staff. She took a piece of masking tape and covered the word Doctors and wrote Nurses over it. Of course, we nurses still let the doctors eat there. We are just that way.

"Good pick up, Steele." Mary says as she looks at the X-ray and the patient. "Let's stick in a chest tube." I nod. I have all the equipment at the bedside waiting for her.

"Steele, would you do me a favor and have someone beep my stupid-ass intern and see if she is interested in doing some of this ucky stuff we call medicine."

"Sure, who's on with you tonight?"

"Bebe."

"Oh give me a fucking break," I say out loud looking up the heavens for some answers. "Bebe Wunderlind is one of the stupidest things God ever put on the face of this earth."

"And ugly too," Mary says.

"Very."

"Stupid and ugly are not her only redeeming qualities. I understand that she is also a virgin."

"Thank you Sweet Jesus." Mary whistles from the bottom of her soul.

Dr. Wunderlind is incredulous when I call her. She cannot believe a nurse is telling her to get up to the ICU. Well, I do speak the language you know. She snorts and says my ass is in a sling when she gets to the unit. No, I say, I would never be put in a sling while on duty. I'm a professional. Slings are for after hours only. I make a mental note to get in touch with my inner kink.

Fifteen minutes later she flies into the unit as if directed by Fellini. Deranged, angry, and totally out of control. Mary Butler and I are done with the inserting the chest tube. Mr. Valentine is stable by the time she arrives and my mind drifts back to Linda Harper.

"Grand of you to show Dr. Wunderlind," snaps Mary Butler as she puts in the last stitch to hold the tube against the chest wall. I cut the thread and start packing the dressing.

Bebe never gets the point unless it is imbedded in her head. "Do you know that this little nurse had the balls to call me and wake me up!"

"Beauty sleep will not help at this stage of the game," I muse. I secure the dressing and listen to Mr. Valentine's lungs. All is good.

Mary Butler tries to bite her tongue to stop herself form laughing. I go for broke taking my stethoscope from my ears and say, "Oh I am sorry doctor, but I thought you knew what you looked like."

Bebe's nostrils flare and I brace myself for her onslaught. What will her aim be? My being gay? My being a male? My being a nurse? My being a gay male nurse?

"Listen you fucking queer nurse boy!" she screams. Ding! Ding! Ding! She went for the gold and took all three shots in one volley.

"I could have your queer ass!" Her chicken neck is straining as her eyes bug out.

"Bebe honey," Mary Butler says calmly, "I doubt that there are that many mind-altering substances on the planet for Mr. Steele to give you his hot ass." Mary Butler pats my butt and winks at me.

I watch as the pressure in Bebe's eyes hits an all-time world record. She is about to spit and explode.

"Now," says Mary Butler, "I am willing to overlook your antigay slur this one time Dr. Wunderlind because that is just the kind of lesbian I am. However, when an ICU nurse calls, you move your butt up here fast. They have been doing this a lot longer than you have, you jackass." Mary blows me a kiss and I catch it.

Bebe is stunned into silence. I look at Mr. Valentine and am sure he is plotting this episode into the basis of a new musical.

"Got it Bebe?!" booms Mary Butler.

"Yes," she croaks back.

"Good, now get lost!" She leaves in her usual dither.

Mary and I continue with the final clean up of Mr. Valentine. As I place a new sheet under his butt I look at Mary.

"Hey Mary, I didn't know you were gay?"

"I'm not Steele. I'm bi."

Well, there you go.

I give report to the night shift in three minutes flat. It is obvious that I want out and no one better make me repeat myself or ask questions. I stare down the room with my evil queen look. No one dares to even look at me.

As I dart out the door one of the night nurses yells, "Well I sure hope he is worth it!"

I turn around and say with glee, "Actually tonight it is a *she.*"

Several people make the sign of the Cross.

My hopes are not dashed. Linda Harper is waiting outside the hospital in a white stretch limo. She is somewhat potted in her appearance. She is hanging out the back passenger-side window with a bottle of champagne and two cigarettes dangling from her mouth.

She spots me. " Did the fucker die?" she yells.

I decide to ignore it and saunter over to the limo. I bend down and look her in the eyes.

"Close but no cigar."

"Fucker!" she slams backward into her seat. "Well get in dammit! We might as well raise hell if that SOB is still ticking!"

The door swings open and I slide in.

"Some days chicken, some days feathers," I say as I spread my hands open. Trying to be caring and honest.

"Yea well, I suppose."

The limo slowly pulls away. "Drink?"

"Sure."

She pours and I realize to my horror that I am still in my stupid-ass white nurse's uniform. I look like an idiot.

We scoff down some bubbly and I inquire to where she is heading.

"Central Park," she says from the lip of her champagne flute, "So I can fuck you."

I gulp. "You serious?" I am only half shocked, but amused.

"You bet I'm serious," she says as she pulls off her dress. "Look at these tits!"

Tits again. This is becoming a recurring issue with me.

"But I am a full-blooded gay man!"

"Oh honey, every fag in the world does me in drag. If it weren't for fags I wouldn't have a fucking career. I'm such a fag icon it will be like fucking a man. Now strip!"

I obey. What the hell at this point?

"Hot damn! Now come to Mama."

On one glass of champagne I am naked and fucking a world-famous movie star in her limo in Central Park. This is my first female fuck.

"Fuck me harder! Harder! Harder!" Linda screams as I go at it. I could not possibly fuck her any harder. I am in actual fear of a penile fracture at this point.

"Honey if I fucked you any harder I would be in your driver's ass!" A pleasant thought after all.

We climax. I pull out. We lay in a heap of pure lust and orgasm. "Where the fuck did you get that body buddy boy?"

"I'm gay. It's genetic."

We drink and fuck for the next five hours. Around 6 a.m. I find myself being driven back to my apartment building. We are still naked. By now the toll of sex, booze, and natural lighting has taken a toll.

I am asleep in the comfort of my own bed when the phone rings. I am trying to remember who I am. In fact, where I am. I notice that no international star of stage and screen is lying beside me. Good, I think. But I do wonder what happened to Linda Harper, and how the hell did I get home. Must be the magic of having servants.

I ponder my desire for my own household staff as the phone continues to drill inside my head. If I had a butler I would not be subject to this nonsense. If I had a butler I doubt I would be lying in a studio apartment with a hangover strong enough to be considered an independent nation.

The first wave of post-partying nausea floods over me. The goddamn phone will not stop ringing. By now I thought it would have just given up.

With my mind clearing the only thing I can think of is that my brother is calling to tell me my mother has died. Then I remember I am an only child. Relief.

I pick up the phone. It is Gloria. "Steele, do not ask questions. Do not say no. Just get your sorry ass over to the unit now." The words are being stammered out and they cannot be denied.

"But Gloria," I attempt as I stare down at my body and feel the puke rise from my guts.

"No buts buddy. Get here. Now!"

The phone goes dead. I pray for the same fate. No such luck.

I puke and shower within an amazing five minutes and head out the door. I feel like shit.

The elevator ride up to the unit is almost more than I can endure. Five little old ladies who wear their perfume like a badge of honor surround me. I can actually see fumes rising from their bodies. I try to be a gentleman and not vomit. My mother would be so proud.

The horde of little old ladies also talks nonstop. They are playing "I have been sicker than the person we are going to visit" game. I try not to listen. I try to zone out. I hear snatches of their conversation and think about suicide as I lean back against the wall and turn green.

"So, I say to Estelle, cheer up for crap's sake. It is just a couple of tubes in your belly. For cryin'out loud when I was in the hospital I had tubes out my butt!"

"I had them in my vagina!"

"The bastards took my vagina!"

"At least you had a vagina to take!"

I close my eyes hard and try not to visualize. I fail.

I walk into the unit trying not to look at the cousin of death with visions of vagina-less women dancing in my head. I see a mass of people. Lots of suits. Something big has happened. I see some nurses from the day shift crying. I see people yelling. I see a mess. I freeze. I have no idea what is going on.

Gloria spies me and raises one eyebrow. It speaks volumes. I am not to be a wiseass. This is no time for jokes.

"I knew I could count on you Steele," Gloria says as she guides me into a stock room.

"What is going on?" I say as a nice opening line.

"You are not going to believe it." Considering I just came in from fucking a female superstar in her limo while drinking heavily for hours I think Gloria is off her mark. I would believe in anything right now. Decent Republicans and Nazis with a sense of rhythm even.

"They dropped him in front of his parents."

I am trying to make sense of this all. "Drop who?" I pause. "Or is it whom?"

"Who, whom, what the fuck!" Gloria screams. "Those two assholes turned a kid over in the Stryker frame without locking it and he fell flat on his face."

"Yikes!"

"Yea, well, thank God he was already paralyzed from the neck down!" Gloria says as she throws a clipboard at me just missing my head. I am impressed with my reflexes considering my condition.

Gloria falls heavily into a chair. "Sorry Steele."

"It's okay. I understand."

What I am trying to understand is how two professional nurses take a paralyzed teenage boy and put him on a Stryker frame to turn him on his belly and forget to lock the damn thing. The poor bastard must have fallen like a brick, unable to protect himself. No wonder the unit is in an uproar. There is enough drama being generated to stage an opera.

"Gloria, may I ask a simple question?"

"Sure."

"Why am I here? Why did you call me?"

"Don't be an ass. To take care of the kid that fell. You think I am going to trust him to anyone else right now?!"

Oh crap.

I change and drink enough mouthwash to catch a slight buzz from it. Gloria introduces me to the family of the kid that fell. The Smiths are actually a lot calmer than I was anticipating. I would have been bat-shit crazy if I were them. Gloria sings my praises as the most competent nurse in all of Manhattan. I am trying not to puke or remember my night with Linda Harper and get a hard-on in front of them. An erect penis right now would be bad form I tell myself.

Tommy Smith is an eighteen-year-old kid who got drunk and dove into a swimming pool without any water in it. He literally broke his neck. Unfortunately, he did not die. He will now spend the remainder of his days totally paralyzed from the neck down with a tracheotomy and strangers taking care of him. I cannot imagine a worse hell.

But before he can even get to the point of his living hell he has to deal with the fact that he has a newly fractured nose and chipped teeth due to the asshole move on the part of the two nurses who forgot to lock the Stryker frame.

I have been sent to provide care and act as a calming influence. I am trying to pull it all together. All I want to do is puke. I think about Harry and Carmella and wonder how in the hell they would handle this situation. Well, in all reality, they never would have answered the phone so neither of them would have been here in my shoes. Harry and Carmella both have the ability of not being anally compulsive. I curse my mother for her toilet training techniques.

Tommy's face looks like a pancake. His nose is splattered against his face and his eyes are dazed. Underneath the trauma you can see one handsome kid.

Tommy cannot talk due to the tracheal tube in his neck that allows him to breathe. Normally, he mouths his words but he isn't in the mood right now. I totally get it. While everyone is screaming about lawyers and such I look at the kid in the bed. He is in pain, mad, scared, and in need of relief.

After gently washing his face and assessing him I tell him it is time for a nap. He raises his eyebrows at me as if to question my sanity. Not a bad judge of character I must admit.

I leave the cubicle with his mother guarding him like only a mother can, and return with a syringe full of morphine. I slip the needle into the IV tubing and give him three milligrams. As soon as the drug hits him he smiles. He is off to dreamland. He looks restful. His mother takes a deep breath. As she strokes his forehead I drop him another two milligrams. I close the curtains and let him and his mom get some much-needed quiet time.

Outside the circus continues. I ask Gloria if the show can be moved out of the unit. It is time for Tommy, and not to mention the other patients, to rest. Nothing is going to be settled in the heat of the moment.

Gloria does her best and moves the brawling band out into the hallway. A calm falls over the unit. I make sure Tommy is okay and stable and talk to the doctor. Nothing more to do. Rest now. Plastic surgery when stable.

I ask Mrs. Smith if she would like a cup of coffee.

"I suppose that would work. However, a Valium and a Bloody Mary seem more appropriate at this point."

I smile. "Sorry, I am not a licensed bartender. But I have dated several."

She smiles and sits back.

I go for the coffee.

We sit in the dim nurse's station and drink coffee and not say much to each other. We can both see into Tommy's cubicle and all is calm at last. Our talk is gentle.

"How are you coping with all of this?" I ask Mrs. Smith.

"I'm okay. I used to be a nurse like you. Then I got married and became a rich lady from the 'burbs. I miss my nursing career." Mrs. Smith sighs and looks sad. "Now I have Tommy and get to be a nurse again while my husband escapes into his work on Wall Street and the distance between us grows." She pauses heavily. "Sorry for the true confessions."

"Confession if good for the soul," I lamely reply.

Mrs. Smith sips her coffee. "So where did you go to nursing school Steele?"

I tell her.

"Oh my God! So did I!"

"You're kidding!"

We both laugh. I am happy that she can laugh now.

"Tell me," Mrs. Smith says, "is that lunatic who taught psych still there. The one with red lipstick smeared across her face liked Bozo on a drunken binge?"

"Ohmygod!" I cannot believe this. "You actually had the same mad woman I had!'

"She was totally nuts when I had her. God, she must be a real mess by now!"

I begin to tell her about the Mr. A-bomb incident when I notice a slight slowing of Tommy's heart rate on his monitor.

"Shit!" I say as I run into the cubicle. Mrs. Smith runs right behind me. It must take all of three seconds to get to Tommy. His heart rate is now almost gone. He is blue.

"Code Red!" I yell. What the hell happened here? No one is responding. Where the fuck is everyone?

Mrs. Smith says calmly, "I'll bag him while you do compressions."

"Got it." I climb onto the bed and feel for Tommy's breast bone and place my hands. Mrs. Smith tilts her son's head just so and kisses him before she hooks up the Ambu bag to his trach and begins pumping in the much-needed oxygen. By now the code team has arrived.

It is organized bedlam. I am trying to make sense out of what is going on and run the code. People are screaming. The confusion is coming to a climax. I hear a voice say: "He must have thrown a fat embolism." I suddenly realize it is Mrs. Smith. She is still bagging oxygen into her son. I look at her.

"I can do that for you," I say.

"No thanks. I feel more useful here." She is acting like a pro and I am wondering how in the hell she is managing it. Gloria tries to take over for her but Mrs. Smith just pushes her out of the way. No one seems to notice.

The code continues for half an hour. Tommy is not responding at all. He has never regained a heartbeat or spontaneous respiration. I am looking at Mrs. Smith. She must know that there is very little hope. I am trying to figure out how to let her know.

My mind drifts. I have never been in this kind of situation before.

"Time to call it." I hear this and stare up at Mrs. Smith. She is the one who just spoke.

"Hey! I call the end of the code when I see fit," says some faceless resident.

"Sorry buddy," Mrs. Smith says. "I outrank you."

"And who the fuck are you?" The hapless resident stammers.

Mrs. Smith's eyes turn icy cold. "I am his FUCKING mother!"

By now I am standing in the middle of the doorway. I know life does not get much more complicated than this and I am at a loss.

Mrs. Smith continues to stare and a unique silence comes over the unit. The only sounds are the gentle pumping of air from the other ventilators and the soft beating sounds of the cardiac monitors.

The seconds pass like hours. Finally, Mrs. Smith says very calmly. "I would truly appreciate it if everyone would leave expect for Mr. Steele." She looks down at Tommy. "We have to spend some time with my son and get him ready."

Wordlessly, the cubicle empties out. There is not so much as a whisper. As the last of the code team leaves I quietly close the door and draw the curtains around the windows. Mrs. Smith reaches up and clicks off Tommy's respirator and cardiac monitor.

I do not want to interrupt her in her thoughts but I move in a little closer.

My voice is shaky and it feels like I am shouting in the silence. "I'm sorry."

Without looking away from her son she says, "I know." After a pause. "And, thanks."

I move to her side of the bed and put my hand on her arm. She has started to disconnect all of the various tubes sticking out of Tommy.

"You know, I can do this," I say. Mrs. Smith looks at me gently.

"I know. But I want to. After all, I was there for the glory of his birth." Her eyes fill. "It only seems natural that I be here for his death."

Both of us cry softly as we clean up Tommy and place him in a shroud. Only after the ordeal of postmortem care is done does Mrs. Smith speak.

"All my years as a nurse I never got used to death. I thought that's what made me a good nurse. Then I drifted off to the suburbs with a rich husband and charities to occupy my time. Maybe Tommy and his accident were my wake-up call."

I look up at her.

"You know, Steele, I think it may be time for me to reenter the world of the living. Time to skip all the wine-filled lunches and silly committee meetings. Their only purpose is to make us feel like we are doing something worthwhile."

"What do you really want to do?"

"I want to be you. I want to go back into nursing."

"You are already back," I said. "I have never seen such courage in nursing as I did today. Not many of us could have done what you did for Tommy."

"Bullshit. You do it everyday."

The next few days are spent in sorrow. I am beginning to wonder how much pain any one nurse can take. Gloria tells me to relax. It is a good sign that death still bothers me. When it stops being an issue it is time to leave. I know she is right but I still feel like shit.

Carmella and Harry offer their usual brand of support that includes snide comments and alcohol. Both are greatly appreciated. However, even the anesthesia of the alcohol is not making the pain subside. I am slowly coming to the conclusion that I need another change. I examine my life once again. I am married to my job but have no college degree. I cannot go anywhere without one. I do not have a boyfriend. The only men I meet are in bars and end up leaving me for Jesus. My mother is pretending to be Jewish and living in Westchester. My best friends are nuts. I have explored heterosexual sex and found it lacking except for the fact that it was a star fuck. My new friends are as nuts as my old ones. Life is good. Life is bad.

Tommy's death leaves me with some unsettled energy. I decide to tackle the hospital's uniform policy in the ICU. Why the hell are we wearing whites? We should be in scrubs which would make life a lot easier. Instead we look like relicts from central casting for Dr. Kildare. I call Daisy McQueen. She answers her own phone.

"McQueen here," she says briskly.

"Steele here," I reply. "I need to see you."

"Fine, I am in my office," she says and hangs up.

She is certainly not one for idol chitchat.

When I get to her office I see that her sense of fashion is still firmly frilly. Today she looks like a linebacker in drag. She is a big, tall, masculine woman who consciously selected a purple dress, a lemon lime ruffled shirt, and red blazer. When she turns around I notice the earrings. They are long dangling balls that I suspect are used on New Year's Eve in Times Square. I remind myself that I am here to talk about the dress code with someone who looks like the losing end of a taffy pull. I sure do know how to pick my battles.

"Daisy," I say pushing down any primeval urge to comment on her outfit. Maybe I should introduce her to my mother? "We need to change the dress code for the unit."

"You are here to talk fashion with me?" Daisy says as she sweeps her hands over her clothes. "I thought you were smarter than that!"

She throws her head back and snorts a laugh of sorts. The earrings swing with such force I am fearful that they are going to blacken both of her eyes.

"It is not about fashion. It is about comfort and better patient care."

"Now why would nursing administration be at all interested in those things Steele? We are bureaucrats. We don't give a fig or a fuck about patient care. We are strictly here to keep our jobs and do nothing." She snorts which sends her earrings into perpetual motion.

I make a mental note to remember the basic principles of nursing administration should I ever be tempted to cross over.

"I think we should have the option of wearing scrubs since it would . . ."

"And give up your virginal allegiance to Flo?"

"Well, it is not like I actually knew her."

"We are supposed to show our devotion to our founding mother by wearing white, pretending to be virgins, and demonstrate our constant sorrow of her passing symbolized by the black bans on nursing caps."

"You know, I think it is more important what a nurse puts *in* her head than what she puts *on it.*"

"Excellent point!" Daisy says as she stands up. "Scrubs it is then."

"That's it?"

"What the fuck Steele. None of these old broads down here would ever dream of going to where we keep the patients. They will probably die or retire and never know anything happened."

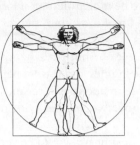

PART FOUR

I ask Gloria to put me in the Open Heart Unit for the next few weeks. I need to be somewhere that I can be useful but not get involved. Open-heart surgery is a critical care nurse's dream. For the most part, patients come in deathly ill and you get to play with them and make them better. The nice part is that within two or three days they are sitting out of bed eating the hospital version of gruel and enjoying life. Before you can even know their name without looking it up they are shipped out to a step-down unit where the real nursing care gets done. All the glory and very little pain for us ICU folks.

I have not been in the Open Heart Unit for months and have not kept up with the gossip so I was surprised to find an old timer lying in cubicle A. He had been in the ICU for months and was beginning to root. Sigh. I know I will get him as my patient. The other nurses have had their fill of him. Time to throw fresh meat his way and I am to be the main course.

Before my mind can kick into a state of denial the evening head nurse approaches me. Jane Eddings is a fairly unkempt woman hovering in her forties without much to cling to. Her glasses are big and round and held together by surgical tape. Her hair has lost any luster it may have once had and is teased up and lacquered down. She has the annoying habit of letting her glasses sit on the tip of her nose which mandates that she crinkle her nose with every word. Once you get over the age of six this is no longer cute. It becomes just damn annoying to the rest of the world. I have to stick my hands in my lab coat pockets to prevent me pushing up Jane's glasses and telling her to stop it.

I make a mental note to be more tolerant of fools. Jane adds an eye squint to the nose crinkling and I make another mental note to forget being more tolerant. I have my limits.

"So, Steele, we finally get our hot little hands on you," Jane announces with some hidden joy. She giggles and pushes her glasses up which just slide down to the tip of her nose in about two seconds.

"Yup." I decide I will overwhelm her with my wit and conversational skill.

"So as the new guy in the unit we would be very interested in your stellar nursing assessment of Mr. Spencer. He has been with us for several months and a fresh pair of eyes may be what he needs." Jane is rambling, and I notice that her lips are dry and cracked. Obviously, the concept of moisturizing is lost on her.

I glance over at the patient and realize what he needs is a ticket to heaven. He looks like hell. Actually, as I look at him more closely, I realize that he does not look sick, but angry. Totally pissed off. Hmm, I think I am going to like him.

Jane is talking. I am asking myself why is she talking. Then I realize she is giving me report on the patient. I try to refocus and pay attention. But it fails. I will just read his chart and catch up on all the details later. I am sure his chart is full of insight and will read like a novel. As my mind continues to drift I hear Jane say something that brings me back into the world.

"He was done by 007 several months ago and has not had an easy post-op course. He has coded twice and now is a mess with a bunch of metabolic issues. He really is a nursing nightmare from the stand . . ."

I drift back into the conversation. "007?" I ask. I am not sure what she means.

Jane's nose and eyes form a stupid laugh. "Oh, that is our little nickname for Dr. Hester. You know, 007. James Bond. Licensed to kill."

Not exactly the moniker I would want.

She continues, "Peter Hester was once a great cardiac surgeon but time and tragedy have caught up with him. He is nearly seventy years old and no longer has the physical skills needed to do the fine work of heart surgery. Also, his daughter was killed in a car crash about three years ago and he just never got over it."

"Damn him for that," I say. How in the hell does one get over that?

Jane continues on and I now see that my little plan for some noninvolved patient care has backfired. I plan to bitch slap Gloria later for letting me go.

"I also may need you to help out tonight in the CCU. The charge nurse called in sick and I am covering. Thankfully, there are only two patients but you never know with those fresh heart attacks. They can sour real fast." She says this with a sense of giddy anticipation. This is just great, I think. I am going to have to break my back for the patient nobody wants in the Open Heart Unit and be expected to run a code in the coronary care unit if needed. Today is not even about chicken or feathers. It is about getting fucked.

Instead of getting my professional nose out of joint I just shrug. This one little incident has solidified my determination to get my bachelor's degree. I will start my crusade for an education in the morning.

Jane flits away and I take a deep breath and head for Mr. Spencer. My eyes do a sweep of the room to make sure every drip is dripping and all is right with the critical care world. All seems fine. It is a typical ICU cube with more machines and odors than most car plants.

I walk over to the patient. "Good afternoon, Mr. Spencer, my name is Steele and I am going to be your nurse for the next eight hours."

Mr. Spencer slowly opens his eyes and makes some nominal contact with me. I feel a slight surge of excitement. Maybe I can be of help here. Bring him back. Nurse him to health. As my mind races to being crowned the next Cherry Ames Mr. Spencer spits in my face.

"Oh good," I say. "So the lines of communication are open." I wipe the spit off my cheek and walk out of the cubicle to be met by Jane.

"So how did it go?"

"He spit on me."

"Good. That means he likes you."

"So if he shits on my head do we get married?"

"I thought that already happened to you?"

There are no secrets in the ICU. Only lies that have not been made reality yet.

I spin myself into a huff and go off to get Jack Spencer's chart to bone up on his case. I take his chart and sit at the nurse's station and begin to read. It is like a textbook of what not to do in medicine and nursing. First, this poor bastard had a surgeon beyond his prime which meant he spent too many hours on the operating room table while on bypass. The heart-lung machine is no one's friend when you stay on it for hours on end. The brain begins to fry and the body fails. It can knock the hell out of the kidneys. Sure enough, Jack needed to be dialyzed for several weeks until his blood pressure was stable enough to keep his kidneys functioning on their own. He was also given a trach and placed on a ventilator for at least two months. He has only been breathing supplemental oxygen through his trach for about three weeks. A small, but promising step to recovery.

I continue to look over his chart and finally see what Jane meant by him being a nursing nightmare. He had a ton of medical problems but they were being slowly addressed. However, his nursing problems were a mile long and not being attended to with any degree of consistency. From reading his chart and my two-minute interaction with him I figured he was depressed, disorientated, and more than likely severely malnourished.

My hunch is that it is time to pull out as many tubes as possible and reintroduce him to the world. My mind is going over what this guy needs and I begin to make some notes to discuss with the resident. I am halfway through my list when a firm hand grasps my shoulder.

I glance up and see God. Okay, not God per say, but a godlike figure. In the reflection of the cubicle glass I see a handsome and well-built man. His face is clear, square, and queer. No straight man could ever be that pretty. His scrubs accent every muscle fiber of his body. I start to get a hard-on when I realize that I will have to stand up eventually and the tenting of my scrubs would be a dead giveaway. I try to think awful thoughts to help shift from lust to dust. Nothing helps. In a matter of three seconds I am rock hard. Thank God I have on my lab coat.

"Excuse me," the godlike creature speaks in a slight Southern draw that I immediately fall in love with. "Are you the nurse taking care of Mr. Spencer tonight?"

"Hmmm. Yup." I am becoming disarmingly nonverbal.

"Great. I am Storm." He says as he sticks his hand out to shake. I attempt to get up. My penis is nearly ripped out of my groin. This time pain is a friend and my dick goes limp from sheer shock. "I'm the new open-heart resident and I would like to discuss his care with you."

My mind races to retrieve all the appropriate social interactions I know I should be doing but all I can come up with is, "Swell. Some days chicken, some days feathers."

"Exactly. And I think Mr. Spencer has had too many days of feathers."

Jesus, he knows what I am talking about. *I* don't know what I am talking about.

He sits in the chair next to mine. "And you are?"

"Oh, sorry Dr. Storm, I was . . ."

"It is just Storm. Don't like all that doctor crap."

"And I am just Steele."

His smile broadens. "Storm and Steele. Has a nice ring to it."

I lean back in my chair. This is going to be very interesting.

Without even trying I launch into the finer details of care of Mr. Spencer. I have spent all of two minutes with the patient and only twice that reviewing his chart, and I sound like I have been working him up for grand rounds. I even impress myself when I get to his albumin level and his need for aggressive nutrition. Where the hell is this coming from? Can lust make me smart? No, if that was the case I would picking up my second Nobel Prize in medicine by now.

Storm and I go back and forth on Mr. Spencer for the next fifteen minutes. He is impressed with my understanding of the case and I am impressed with his need to heal Mr. Spencer.

Storm's beeper cuts into our conversation. He is being stat paged to the CCU. I look across the way and can see Jane on the phone. Storm just rushes over to see what is wrong. I follow. Mr. Spencer is sleeping and stable, and I can watch his monitors from across the way.

Storm and I hit the CCU before Jane can even put down the phone. She seems startled at our quick response.

"You rang?" Asks Storm.

"Bed three. Crushing chest pain. Not responding to protocol of sublingual nitro and morphine IV push. T-waves are looking like tombstones. I am alone here."

Great. Some patient decides to have an acute heart attack in the coronary care unit while I am lusting for this hunk of a doctor. I just don't think patients have any consideration for my needs at times.

"Well, that is certainly rude. I hate it when patients do not know what treatment is supposed to work," Storm says as he strides into the room.

"Think she would have read the cardiology text like the rest of us," I quip back.

The patient looks like shit. She is an unbecoming shade of gray with a firm grip on the death rattle. She is clutching the bed's side rails as if she expects turbulence.

"Storm and Steele here to take care of you."

"The pain is . . ." she begins to say.

"Jane. Med keys please, " I say as I walk out of the room to get more morphine. Jane tosses me the keys and I return in about a minute. Storm has turned up the patient's oxygen and is trying to get a blood pressure reading.

I hold up five fingers to indicate that I plan on giving her five milligrams of the morphine in her IV.

He nods ascent. I slip the needle in the tubing and push the painkiller in slowly but steadily. The patient pinks up and her breathing becomes easier.

The patient is stabilizing. Nothing like a little morphine to dilate the heart vessels and get some blood to the pump.

I suddenly remember that I had a hard-on only moments ago. I do a quick check to make sure it has gone away. Thankfully it has.

Storm and Jane continue to assess the patient and regulate her drips and get a stat EKG. I do a quick tour of the other patient and all is calm. I poke my head back into the room and tell them I am heading back to the Open Heart Unit.

"Call if you need anything," I say.

"Sure will," says Storm. "I'll stop by when I am done here."

I smile hoping that I am doing my best Cary Grant. However, I expect that I am more Natalie Wood.

I return to the unit and go into Mr. Spencer's cubicle. He is a mess. His face is turned up into a ball of rage and the sheets are in a bunch. Not that I blame him.

I stand at the foot of the bed and look him right in the eyes. "Look Jack. I am going to be honest with you here. You got screwed. I do not know the full story but it is clearly the short end of the stick."

Some light dances from his eyes.

"I can't do anything about what has happened but I can help you with what will happen. However, I need your help." With that speech he looks directly at me and honks up a bolus of phlegm from his trach and sends it across the room in my direction. I duck and it hits the wall.

"I will take that for a yes."

I am gathering what supplies I need to take care of Mr. Spencer when Storm comes back into the unit.

"May I have a moment Steele?" he says.

"Sure."

"Would you like to have dinner some night this week? Are you free on Friday night?"

I try not to jump into his arms and ask him to marry me. "A small handling fee always applies."

"You are something," he says as he smiles.

"Like a date?" I manage to sputter.

Storm becomes flustered. "I assumed you were gay like me and that we made a connection. Sorry if I was mistaken."

Again with the mistaken identity for heterosexual. I really need to work on this.

"Not a mistake at all. Not a straight bone in my body. Actually I did it once but I was drunk and she was famous."

"Isn't that the line most straight guys say about sex with a man?"

"I do things in reverse."

"How about I pick you up Friday at eight?"

I spend the rest of the evening with Mr. Spencer. He is my new mission in life. Okay, outside of getting into this new doctor's pants. I plan to make him well or kill him in the trying. Of course, snagging a date with a hot Southern doctor without even trying has made me a little lighter in my loafers than normal. My main decision is whom do I call first? Carmella or Harry? I decided on Harry since I can rub it in with more glee. What else are best friends for?

Spending the evening planning out Mr. Spencer's care is a welcome challenge. I come to the conclusion that he has become one of the forgotten souls of intensive care. He has been here too long and just became part of the furniture. No one is really paying him any attention.

I outline my plan of nutrition, rest, counseling, and time reorientation to Jane. My goal is very simple but will take a great deal of will and enforcement. I want Mr. Spencer to get out of bed every day and have some physical therapy, have a dietary consult, place a clock and calendar in his cubicle, and have one-on-one conversations with the staff every day about what is going on in the world. The ICU becomes a black pit for most people. You can fall into a deep depressing hole. Patients are simply dropped there and time comes to a halt. There is no such thing as real sleep. People poke at you twenty-four hours a day. You never know when it is raining or if the sun is up. Your privacy goes out the window along with your dignity.

Jane is impressed. I am impressed. The only person not impressed is, of course, Mr. Spencer. He just wants to be left alone. He is very tired of all the nonsense and is more than likely hoping to die and be done with it. I need to find a hook to make this guy want to get well. I will ponder this over a much-needed drink with Harry over the phone when I get home.

"So. A doctor?" Harry says.

"Yup."

"You must be proud."

"Very."

"So is this the real reason you went to nursing school? You are just like all those other husband-seeking females. Marry a doctor, move to the 'burbs and have two point five cute towheaded kids?"

"Actually, after my disastrous affair with Myles, I thought I had sworn off doctors. But you know, there is something about this guy that has nothing to do with him being a physician."

"Now we are getting somewhere."

I hear Harry pause and rattle the ice in his glass. I pause to take a sip of my Scotch. I silently thank God for the invention of the phone so I do not have to drink alone in my apartment. Modern conveniences should never be taken for granted.

"Well, I think the bottom line here is Storm is nice."

"Nice? Like in take home to mother nice? Or a nice piece of ass?"

"A nice piece of ass that I want my mother to meet."

"Want some advice?"

Like the word "no" would work here.

"Don't put out on the first date."

I laugh. "Harry, that is so 1950s. Sounds like the Sandra Dee guide to dating."

"Just remember that Sandra always got her man."

I masturbate three times on Friday before my date with Storm to make me as close to Sandra Dee purity as possible. Of course all I do is fantasize about Storm all the time. So much for my plan, and by the time evening rolls around I am eyeing small farm animals. I vow to steady my resolve. I think Harry is right this time. Jumping into bed is not the right thing to do. Of course, I have gone to be bed with strangers for a gin and tonic in the past. However, I decide to be adult this time. Dinner, conversation, and *maybe* a kiss.

At 7:59 I know he is not going to show. I am in the throws of depression. At 8:01 I am fixing myself a double Scotch on the rocks and preparing for a night of self-pity and Judy Garland songs.

At 8:07 the doorbell rings. I down the last of my drink and take a last look in the mirror. If this is a Jehovah's Witness I plan to kill them with my bare hands. I look stunning for a man prepared for a date or homicide. I decide that flexibility is the key to life.

Framed in the doorway Storm is standing in a white button-down shirt, chinos, and sockless penny loafers. He is also holding a bunch of purple tulips.

"Sorry I am late but I had to get you these," he says with a smile as he pushes the flowers toward me.

I smile and hope that Sandra Dee will forgive me as all thoughts of purity empty out of my head. He steps into my apartment and gives me a tentative kiss.

"Hmmm. Scotch. My favorite." Storm says as he pulls me closer tasting my mouth.

"Let me fix you one." I say as I take the flowers from him. Glancing at my watch it has been about fourteen seconds and my resolve to be chaste has totally vanished. However, I remind myself, this is a new record for me.

I place the tulips in a vase in the kitchen like this is a normal activity for me. In fact, I am hoping that he will not notice that the vase is an old glass urinary beaker I snatched from nursing school. I convince myself that many people have vases with urinary volumes etched on the side of them.

We are standing in my railroad of a kitchen and Storm says, "Where did you find this shade of plum. It is great. I have never seen anything like it before." He gazes around admiringly.

"A slave for the finer things," I manage to say and silently thank Judi for her unusual tastes. I hand Storm his drink. I do some quick mental gymnastics and realize this is the first time I am handing a man a drink without it coming from a bartender. Jesus, what the hell do I do now? There isn't any disco to take up the silence.

We sit on the couch and sip our drinks. I suddenly remember that I am suppose to be an adult. Adults having drinks should offer something to eat. I mentally scan my kitchen for something to eat. I can whip up butter and crackers with a side of Fritos.

"Let me get you something to go with that drink," I say as I start to stand up from the couch and wonder what in the hell I am going to come back with.

"You already have," Storm says as he pulls me back down and kisses me. We get lost in each other for a while. When we finally come up for air the ice in our glasses has melted and so has my resolve.

"I have been wanting to do that with you since the first day I started my ICU rotation," Storm says softly.

I blush. What the fuck is happening here? I never blush.

"Really?" I manage to say as my retort.

"Ah, come on Steele," Storm says in that kind Texas voice. "You are smart, hot, and built. Plus I think you are not only a nice guy but a great nurse." He pauses to let it sink in. "You must have had a lot of boyfriends."

"Not really. Been too busy with being a cheap slut." Oh, that ought to win him over. "Actually, I did have one serious boyfriend in nursing school but he left me for Jesus."

"Well, that is impressive. The only man you have seriously dated left you for God."

"Yea, I know. Kind of pisses me off too. It is impossible to be mad at either of them."

"So, you are not seeing anyone right now? No serious boyfriends?"

"Nope," I will remain cool and casual. I will handle this evening like a code in the Unit. High drama under control.

"Then I will have to be on my best behavior in hopes of changing that," Storm grins and turns a little pink in the face.

"Be careful. If my mother gets wind of my dating a doctor you will be stalked until we are married."

He laughs. "So will my father. My mom died years ago and my dad and I are very close. He keeps sending me copies of *The Advocate* with not-so-subtle hints on personal ads he has circled for me to answer."

"My God, my mother fixed me up with a waiter the day I came out to her. He turned out to be in love with everything tragic. I just don't get it. Parents are expected to reject their gay sons, wring their hands in dismay, and have novenas said for our recovery. Instead, we seem to have parents that care and want what is best for us."

Storm gets up and takes my drink. "Let's get dinner and talk. I want to fall head over heals in like with you tonight."

Dinner takes four hours and two bottles of wine. Food magically comes and goes and I do not recall any of it. We talk about everything and hardly anything clinical except to share the war stories of our training. It appears that the health care education field is filled with comic relief no matter what the profession.

"There was this guy in our fourth year of med school who was just plain dumb," Storm says over coffee. "I kind of felt sorry for him. Here we were about to graduate and become physicians and this guy could not pour piss out of a boot. I think his daddy was a big contributor of something. Anyway, one day we were doing a final rotation in surgery. Nothing big. All the bullshit was over. We were just putting in time till we graduated. So this guy, his name was Harold, and I were stitching up leg incisions. I was doing one and he was doing the other. Boring as shit. No one is paying any attention to anyone. So the surgery is over and we go to move the patient onto the stretcher to take her to recovery. You know the drill. On the count of three we all are suppose to lift the patient," Storm pauses now for effect. "When we get the old gal into the air Harold lets out this scream. We all fucking freeze not knowing what the hell is going on. It seems the jerk sewed the sleeve of his OR gown into the patient's groin."

"You are bullshiting me!" I start to laugh.

"Wait, it gets better. Harold is now lying between her legs with his arms stitched to this woman's thigh and his hand is right near her vagina. Next thing we know the patient begins to wake up and buck from the anesthesia. So before any of us could do anything Harold is essentially fingering this old lady while she is asleep. Everyone is laughing, except for the old lady, and trying to do something, but it is too damn funny. By now the patient is practically riding his fist!"

"Holy fucking God! What the hell happened?"

"I think she came."

I spit wine clear across the table onto Storm's shirt.

We laugh and people are beginning to stare us down. I try to regain some control.

"So what happened to Harold?"

Storm just shrugs. "Nothing. He graduated. Went on to become an OB/GYN and I think the old lady set up a scholarship in his name."

We laugh some more.

"You are good to laugh with Steele."

"So are you."

"Let's walk off the wine and go for a drink somewhere."

"Sounds perfect to me."

Storm pays the bill over my protest but reminds me he asked me out.

We are walking up Third Avenue and I say, "So where to for the drink? Auntie Em's?"

"Hell no," Storm says as he flags down a taxi. We climb in and he says, "The Plaza please."

In the cab he places his hand on mine and squeezes. I squeeze back.

I have never been to the Plaza before. I enter as if I do it all the time. Then I remember that I have fucked a Hollywood legend in the back of her limo and this helps me place it into perspective. I look at Storm and my brief deviation to heterosexuality is firmly forgotten.

We are escorted to a table in the Palm Court. A tuxedoed waiter appears from thin air to take our drink order.

"Martini?" Storm suggests.

"Great," I say. In fact I have never had a martini and only know of them from watching *Auntie Mame* 472 times.

"Storm, what in the hell is your first name? I am so used to people calling me Steele that I forget that it is unusual to be known by just one name."

"Promise you won't laugh."

"Nope."

"Gale."

I am about to wet my pants when the drinks arrive. The martinis are enormous and beautiful. I think Auntie Mame would be proud. As the waiter backs away I stare at Storm.

"Your name is Gale Storm?"

"Yup. My parents thought it was cute."

He picks up his martini and I follow suit. He sips. I sip. I decide before the gin hits my stomach that martinis are the elixir of life.

"Gale Storm? As in *My Little Margie?*"

"The very one and the same."

"Well, no wonder your parents are so wonderful about you being gay. I mean, what choice did you have?"

"Exactly," he says picking up his glass.

Over the martinis I find out that Storm is an only child. His mother was a nurse and was killed in a car accident when he was just three. His father is a retired Episcopal priest that never remarried and raised Storm by himself. His passion in life is not critical-care medicine, but to be a happy person. Medicine is just something that he does and is good at but it is not consuming. I tell him my life story as best I can remember it. I try not to make anything up.

Before we are tempted to have a third martini I suggest that it is time to go home. "Let's grab a cab."

We walk past the sleeping security man in the lobby of my building and head up to my apartment. I am calculating that sex will begin in about 8.2 minutes. At my apartment door Storm looks me in the eyes and I melt.

"I hope you had a good time tonight."

"The best," I say. "So, can I ask you in?"

"I better not. I would be all over you in a New York minute."

"And that is bad?"

"The first time we go to bed I want us to make love and not just have sex."

Storm leans into me and kisses me. My back is against the door. He pushes into me deeply. Suddenly, the doorbell rings. We both laugh.

"It appears time is up."

"I am off the whole weekend. Can I cook you dinner tomorrow night at my place?" Storm asks.

"I'd like that."

He kisses me again. This time he holds me in his arms for a very long time.

"What can I bring?" I ask as we fall away.

"I think maybe a toothbrush."

I blush.

"I think you are very special."

"Good night doctor."

"Good night nurse."

Storm backs away and moves down the hall toward the elevator.

I call after him. "Hey, where do you live?"

"Check your pocket!" He says as he disappears into the elevator.

In my back pocket I find a piece of paper. Jesus. I thought he was fondling my ass but he was placing a note in my pants. This is a first. I unfold the piece of paper and see that he has written his address and phone number on it.

I fall into bed and into deep sleep. The only thing that wakes me is the goddamn phone ringing at nine in the morning. It is Carmella.

"So?" she says as I hear smoke exhaling from her lungs.

"So?" I am not going to make this easy.

"Details please."

"I think I am falling in love. We did not sleep together. He is making me dinner at this place tonight. I am bringing a toothbrush. Good-bye." I hang up and unplug the phone before she can call me back. By the time my eyes are closing again I figure she is on the phone to Harry.

Around noontime I roll over and Carmella and Harry are standing at the foot of my bed. I jump up naked.

"Holy fucking hell!" I yell as I leap onto the top of the bed.

"You're right. He does have a nice dick."

"Told you."

"How the hell did you get in here?"

"Security guard let us in. This is what you get when you unplug a phone." Harry says as he holds up the phone cord as evidence.

"Why of course he did. Why wouldn't he let two strangers into my apartment while I am asleep!"

"We are hardly strangers."

Carmella turns her head to Harry. "Just one date with a big-time doctor and he forgets who his dearest friends are. Bet we don't even get invited to the wedding."

I am slowly coming to when I hear another voice. It is Gloria.

"Hey Steele, I have been trying to call you for hours." She says as she looks at my groin. "Nice dick for a white boy, by the way."

I yank a sheet around my waist and stumble out of bed in my highly cherished sleeping alcove.

"What the hell is going on here?" I manage to ask as my mind attempts to focus.

Harry speaks. "We just came to see how your *date* went since you unplugged the phone."

"Did I hear the word date?" Gloria asks.

"Yup. D-A-T-E," Carmella spells.

"Oh come off it. I have had plenty of dates."

"No, Steele. You have had plenty of men," Harry says. "You fuck, but you don't date."

I eye Gloria next. "And you are here because?"

"We need you in the unit."

"No way!"

"We have a celebrity who is coked out of her head and running around trying to snort anything she can get her hands on. So far I think she has inhaled three packets of Sweet 'N Low."

"Before you go any further. I am not working this weekend at all. I have a second date with Storm tonight and there is no way in hell I am going to miss it. And what the hell is a cokehead doing in the ICU if she is not critical."

"Because she is *famous*."

"Oh great. Now the ICU can become a celebrity hangout for addicts."

From the doorway I hear another familiar voice.

"Who's famous?"

In walks my mother who is dressed in a green plaid pantsuit with a ruffled shirt. She looks like a leprechaun from the mafia. Her purse is a white vinyl number that could easily conceal a machine gun.

"You must be Steele's mother. I am Gloria. I work with your son."

My mother takes Gloria's hand gently and says to me. "Yes, my son the big-time nurse who could not even bother to call his mother to tell her he had a *date* with a *doctor*. If it weren't for Harry and Carmella . . ."

"I would still be asleep and not standing here naked with an apartment full of people."

"Some days chicken, some days feathers," my mother says.

"Oh God," I groan.

"Ma, how in the world did you get here? You always said taking the bus and subway makes you crazy but here you are."

"You make me crazy. And I drove."

"You don't have a car."

"I bought one."

"You bought a car? Without telling me!"

"A hot little pink number. Hell, you go out on a date and not tell me."

"It was just a date!"

"Ha!" she says.

"Ha?"

"Ha." That settles that.

I am plotting on which nursing home I can place my mother in and how to kill Carmella and Harry without being caught. I also realize that I am turning bluish from being naked with nothing more than a sheet around my body. No one seems to notice much. They are talking and asking questions of one another. It is only 12:15 in the afternoon and I want a drink.

I stand up and try to get everyone's attention. I fail. Like there was any other choice. Another voice enters the bedlam. It is Storm.

"Hey Steele, I couldn't wait until tonight and got worried when I couldn't get you on the phone." Storm stops dead and surveys the scene. Me wrapped in a sheet looking like hell surrounded by four people in various states of excitement now that *he* has arrived.

"Someone remind me to drop-kick the doorman later," I say to no one in particular.

Silence has come over the assembled and I seize the opportunity.

"Storm, gathered before you is my family of sorts. Gloria you know. She is the diva of ICU and my boss. She is here to get me to come in on my day off and take care of a famous cokehead. I have demurred. Next to Gloria is

Harry. Harry gave me my start in ICU and we have never had sex. Carmella is my oldest friend in the world. She is also a nurse but does not let the caring aspect of the calling get in the way of a good time. I have known Carmella forever." I pause. "Actually, how the hell do I know you? When did we meet?"

"I have always just been."

"Well, of course she has!" My mother adds.

"And that woman happens to be my mother who lives in Parkchester and tells everyone it is Westchester, now owns a pink car of some ilk, and is obviously hoping for a revival of *Finian's Rainbow* by the looks of her get up." My mother beams and twirls around proudly.

I sweep my hand around the room. "Everyone, this is Storm. He does not have a first name. It is forbidden by his religion."

"Howdy," Storm says as he grins. Even in the middle of this mayhem my heart melts.

"Well, howdy right back at you big boy," Harry says with much lust in his voice.

My mother throws her hands in the air and shouts. "Out! Everyone out! My boy has a date!" They all start to head for the hallway. "Come on, I'll drive everyone home," she says as she ushers them out the door. She turns and smiles at me and winks. "Looks just like Sky King."

"Shut the door!" I yell as I try to gather up the bedsheet.

Storm and I are now alone in my apartment. I must look like hell.

"This is not exactly what I envisioned our second date to be like."

"They seem nice."

"Nice and loony."

"Good combination if you ask me."

Storm holds up a shopping bag. "I brought lunch. Champagne and chicken salad!"

"Great," I say and mean it.

"Why don't you get in the shower and I will make myself useful in the kitchen."

"Sounds perfect to me."

I make it to the bathroom and look at myself in the mirror. This must be love because he has not run out the door screaming at the sight of me. My hair is plastered to one side of my head and my eyes are partly glued shut. I make quick absolution of shaving and brushing my teeth and step into a hot shower. I let the water wash over me and give me strength when a glass of champagne is offered through the shower curtain. Storm has chosen my best jelly jars for the bubbly.

"I thought you could use this," Storm says.

I take the champagne and pull back the curtain. He is totally naked. He is built bigger than I am and totally gorgeous.

"May I?"

I step back and let him in. He touches me and brings the glass of champagne to my lips then takes a sip from the other side. I do not think I am breathing.

"I am going to make love to you." And he does.

We spend the next few hours drinking champagne, eating chicken salad sandwiches, and making love. It is incredible.

"What about our date tonight?"

"I think it has already started."

We order in and never leave my apartment for the rest of the weekend.

I return to the unit on Monday and am feeling like a new man. I am falling in love for the first time and it feels great. I remind myself not to rush things. Take your time, my mind says. Of course, I have chosen the china pattern already.

When I get off the elevator Gloria is standing there with a dozen long-stemmed red roses in her arms.

"Miss America I presume?" I say.

"They just came for you hot stuff!"

"What?"

"Seems a certain doctor is truly hot for you," she says as she hands me the flowers. They are beautiful. I look around for a card and find it. It reads: "PLEASE BE MY BOYFRIEND FOREVER."

I am blushing. Gloria is laughing. Suddenly, the big-time TV star who is hiding in the ICU and trying to get detoxed from coke comes running over to me.

"Hey there, flower boy! You carrying any coke?" she says as she opens up her bathrobe and two of the sorriest looking breasts flash into view. I wonder if she has nursed an entire tribe with those things.

"Nice tits," I say in an attempt to be a gentleman and polite. "However, I do not happen to have cocaine on me at this time."

"What the fuck good are you then?" she says as she storms off back into the unit.

"Exactly," I say as I spread my hands. The big-time TV star puts a finger against her nostril and inhales deeply before she stomps back into the unit.

"I should have introduced you, Steele. She is going to be your patient this evening along with Mr. Spencer."

I look Gloria right in her baby browns. "You have got to be kidding."

"I kid you not. In fact I lost my kidding the day I saw your penis and your boyfriend."

"What does my penis and my boyfriend have to do with anything?"

"If I have to explain that to you then maybe he should be *my* boyfriend."

"You know sometimes I think boundaries are a good thing."

"Too late for that now."

I head into the unit. Gloria follows.

I am in the Open Heart Unit and reviewing Mr. Spencer's chart. I have placed my roses in a vase and they look beautiful. I stat page Storm to the Unit. He comes running in breathlessly about eighty-two seconds later.

"What's up? Who's sick?" he stammers.

Without looking up I hold up the card from the flowers he sent me and say, "The answer is yes."

He just grins. "Best stat page I will ever have."

We make plans for later. I promise to molest him in his on-call room for hours.

"The stat page thing was cute," Gloria says.

I just shrug.

"So where do I find the big-time TV star and what do I do for her?" I ask Gloria.

"Not to worry, Steele, she will find you. Officially, she had a bed in the CCU but she is never in it. She spends her time going from room to room trying to find drugs. She has not yet figured out that we keep the good stuff locked up. Last night I found her in the staff bathroom with baby powder and a mirror."

"Great."

"We are supposed to keep her from harming herself and from the public. No one is suppose to know that she is in here for a coke habit. She is the star of a number-one rated late-night soap opera, which I have never seen. However, I understand she is hot shit."

I choose to ignore the bit about keeping out of the public eye. I mean she flashed her tits at me in the hallway a few moments ago so I figure that the jig is up.

"And what about her coke issues? What in the hell are we supposed to do about them in the ICU?"

"The crazy psych nurses come down every shift and do talk therapy with her." Gloria rolls her eyes.

"Psych nurses are generally nuts so that should work out well."

Gloria nods. "I swear they are loonier than their patients." My mind drifts back to Mr. A-bomb and my psych rotation in nursing school. I am not up for this.

I busy myself with Mr. Spencer and he does look a little better. He is actually sitting in a chair and is all cleaned up. I sit on the bed and talk to him and remind him of the correct day and time. I ramble on about some insignificant current event. He sticks his thumbs in his ears and wiggles his hands. I stick my tongue out at him and leave the room.

I make a mental note to act more mature when dealing with critically ill patients. Screw it, I think a moment latter, life is too short to be an adult.

I am placing Mr. Spencer back into bed for the night. I am going to close the drapes in his cubicle and turn off the lights and give him a sleeping pill. I figure he will never heal if he does not get back to a regular schedule. I will have to have a meeting with Dr. Hester and try to get him out of the ICU. He is going to be psychotic if he stays here much longer.

As I pivot him onto the bed I see the big-time TV star's face underneath Mr. Spencer's bed covers. She is holding the sheets around her head like Heidi, the goat herder. She screams "Boo!" and scares the hell out of Mr. Spencer and myself. He lets loose with a stream of farts that could power a Macy's Thanksgiving Day balloon.

I spin him around and land him safely into bed. I barely miss putting his sorry ass on her head. She jumps back.

"What the hell was that about?!" I demand.

"Just trying to liven things up around here." She it taking the headdress off and fanning the fart fumes out of her face.

"Sweetheart," I say without any affection in my voice, "this is an intensive care unit and not a make-believe set. We have enough real-life drama here without you being an asshole."

"I am not an asshole!"

"Yes you are!"

Mr. Spencer looks at her and mouths, "You are a *fucking asshole!*"

She cinches up her bathrobe and heads for the hallway looking for lack-luster Jane.

"I am going to report you!"

"Well, I am going to put you in four-point restraints and medicate the fuck out of you!"

She stops dead. Her eyes gleam. "Would you really?"

Great. Just fucking great, I think to myself.

My shift finally ends and I am weary. I have talked to some of the other nurses and have gotten some advice on where to get my bachelor's degree. I promise myself again that I will tackle this in the morning. I am getting too old for this ICU stuff. Then I remember I am in love and I wash up and head down to the call room where Storm will be sleeping tonight. I feel just like a cheap dime-novel nurse getting ready to pounce on a doctor, and I like the feeling.

When I knock on the door there is no answer so I naturally go in. Storm is not there but has left me a note. "Curing the sick. Will be back soon. I love you. Take off your clothes."

Who am I not follow doctors' orders?

I take off my scrubs and take a quick shower in the tiny bathroom. I climb into the bed and wait. I am reading a boring article in *The New England Journal of Medicine* when there is a knock on the door. I am hoping it is a steward with some cocktails. Before I can answer the door in walks the big-time TV star clearly coked out of her mind. She stumbles into the room and takes a look at me naked in bed.

"What in the holy hell are you doing here?!" I scream.

"I could ask you the same thing!"

"I work here!"

Her eyes get a glint that I do not like. "And what kind of work would that be that requires you to be naked?"

"Missionary work!"

"Missionary position is more like it big boy."

And that is when she begins to laugh and laugh and laugh. She is laughing so hard that her nose starts to bleed. Not a small trickle, mind you, but a big, bloody, cocaine-induced hemorrhage. I stare at her in horror. I am naked in an on-call room waiting for my boyfriend, and the big-time TV star is gushing blood out of her nostrils. Clearly I have made some bad choices today.

I jump out of bed and head for the big-time TV star in my birthday suit. By the time I get to her she is pale. Blood is now flowing out of her nose at a rate I did not think physiologically possible.

"Jesus Christ!" I yell. "How much coke have you done?"

"Not enough."

"By whose standards? Your dealer?!"

I pick up my scrubs and try to hold some pressure on the bridge of her nose. She starts to scream. Blood is now splattered on my naked body and all over the room. My basic instinct tells me that my notion of a romantic evening is not going to happen.

"Will you hold still so I can stop the fucking bleeding!"

She just whimpers louder.

"Where in the hell did you find coke in a hospital?"

As I pinch her nose I page Storm. He calls back in a minute.

"Don't ask questions but please bring ice and nasal packing back to the on-call room."

"Why would that cause me to ask questions?" he says and hangs up. I am now totally in love with him. He understands me.

The big-time TV star is calming down, and I start looking for something to put around my waist. She notices and says, "Honey, don't bother at this point." She pauses and looks between my legs. "Nice dick by the way."

I am beginning to think that my penis should have its own fan club.

I get some cold water and soak the only towel in the room and place it on her face. I am holding her in my arms when Storm walks in. He does not seem surprised.

"I always knew you'd leave me for someone rich and famous," he says.

I shoot him a look of death.

"Fix her goddamn nose while I shower and get some dignity."

"Oh honey," the big-time TV star says, "your dignity left on the early bus."

I stomp in the bathroom and perform a blood-cleansing ritual. I return to the scene of the crime wearing a cloth bath mat tied around my waist. Storm is in midsentence as I walk in.

"You are right," he says. "He *does* have a nice dick."

"Doesn't anybody else want a normal life like me?" I demand.

Not missing a beat they say in one voice, "No."

"My mother is beginning to look sane."

Storm inserts a speculum in her nose to assess the damage. I can see his eyes widen. "Take a look babe," he says to me.

I do as instructed. There is no visible septum separating the chambers of the nose. It has been coked away.

"Well there, young lady," Storm says. "It seems that you have lost all the cartilage in your nose."

"Lost it?" Cranks the big-time TV star. "Where in the hell could I have lost it?"

"One need not look further than your last line of cocaine," I suggest.

"Oh fuck off dick boy!" she says.

"Now you hang on there missy," Storm says. "That dick boy is my boy-friend."

The big-time TV star just rolls her eyes.

"So where did you get the coke tonight?" I ask trying to interject some sanity.

"The operating room of course."

"Stands to reason," nods Storm.

"You just walked into the OR and took cocaine out of the medication cabinet?"

"Of course not. I had to ask for the keys."

We both just stare at her.

"Hospitals are very lax you know. All you have to do is put on some scrubs and a mask and no one ever questions you." The big-time TV star pauses thoughtfully. "Be a great place for a murder."

Storm and I wince at the truth.

Before Storm escorts her back to the unit he tosses me a fresh pair of scrubs.

"God only knows what can happen before I get back, " he says. "It seems like every time I walk in on you you happen to be naked in a room full of people. No more nude scenes until *I* get back."

The rest of the evening remains uneventful except for the lovemaking. I fall asleep in his arms and do not wake up until morning. I am happy.

The next day as I am getting ready for work in my apartment I wonder what the hell *was* the big-time TV star doing in the on-call room?

The phone rings. It is my mother.

"So?"

"So?" I respond.

"Well?" she counters.

"Well what?" I reply.

"If you don't tell me what is going on with you and the doctor I am going to get in my big pink car and come for a visit and stay for a month!" She is serious.

"Ma, why do you do this?"

"You are my only child. I am a widow. What the hell else am I going to do?"

"You could try rejecting me because I am gay and never talking to me again!"

"The easy way out! Never!"

I tell her everything.

I decide to be an adult. I tell Storm I have fallen deeply in love with him in a short period of time. I totally expect him to run away or join the priesthood. He just looks at me and says, "Marry me."

I try to respond but it appears the gift of speech has left me. Storm never diverts his gaze. He is waiting for an answer. Jesus Christ.

"I love you," I say.

"That is not an answer to the question."

"Would 'yes' work?"

He breaks out into a broad smile and hugs me.

"I love you too."

We kiss.

Storm and I decide to keep our relationship quiet for the time being. This translates into everyone in the entire hospital knowing about it in less than twenty-four hours. I even get a call from Daisy McQueen offering her congratulations.

"Steele, Daisy McQueen here," the voice commands on the other end of the phone. I figure that I have committed some sin of nursing and am about to be punished. I note to work on my self-esteem.

"Hello Daisy," I manage to stutter.

"I hear that you and Storm are an item and I just wanted to say 'nice going there buddy'."

"Gee, thanks." What the hell is this?

"Everyone in nursing administration is a dyke. Nice to see some gay men around for balance," she says and hangs up the phone.

Why do I even bother, I wonder? Then I realize that I don't bother at all, so it all works out.

Cohabitation bliss has to be put on hold as I get back to the reality of ICU nursing. My game plan not to get involved with anymore patients backfires as I care for Mr. Spencer. Since I started on my plan of nutrition and counseling he dramatically improves. He does not look as angry and has not flung phlegm at me in the past thirty-six hours. Some of his tubes have come out and tonight I plan on taking him for walk in the hallway. I calculate that he has not been outside of his cubicle in months. The only remaining problem is "Dr. 007." It appears that Dr. Hester has lost all interest in Jack's case and finds him annoying at this point. I cannot get him to pay attention. Storm cannot get him to pay attention. So I figure it is up the patient.

I gently tell Jack that it is time for him to speak up. He needs to have his trach removed and get the hell out of the unit. Time for some rehab then hit the beach, have a martini, eat a steak, and get laid. The order of which is optional I inform him.

Just as we are slowly walking down the hallway I see the big-time TV star talking with Jane in the CCU. There is something odd about the two of them together. A crazed actress and dizzy nurse is a combination that makes me nervous.

As I am pondering which one of the two is loonier, Dr. Hester walks around the corner. He is totally befuddled as usual.

Jack stops in his tracks and looks at Hester. I figure that this in not going to be a pretty scene and I brace myself.

Much to my surprise Jack just farts as the good doctor passes by and starts to giggle. The giggle turns into a belly laugh with more gas being passed out his butt. I cannot help but burst out laughing also.

Jane and the TV star come out of the CCU to see what is going on and start to laugh at the sight of us. I cannot figure out what is funny exactly but we are all laughing fools. Dr. Hester stops and turns around. Jane, myself, big-time TV star, and Jack are nearly passing out from laughing. Jack gives Dr. Hester the finger. The good doctor returns the gesture.

The big-time TV star wets herself from laughing and we continue our walk. Jane and the big-time TV star go back into the CCU. I figure that I will be fired within the next twenty-three minutes.

My hopes for unemployment go unrewarded. I am promoted to evening assistant head nurse for the entire critical care unit. This officially means that Jane and I are running the show for the evening shift. I suspect she is nuts and would have made a good psych nurse. I am trying to understand this foolish administrative move when Storm reminds me that the extra money will help with my going back to school. I hate people being reasonable while I am in a dither.

As the assistant head nurse my responsibilities include saving the world, doing the scheduling, taking care of patients when someone calls in sick, and putting up sharing an office with Jane. For all of this I make an extra grand a year. It's a stepping-stone they all tell me. You will never climb the ladder of success without going up the first rung. Bullshit. I feel like I just stepped in shit.

I am making rounds in all the critical care units making sure everyone is happy. No one is, of course, and I cannot do anything about it. So I just smile and lie. I think I am beginning to get the hang of management.

In the CCU Jane is once again alone covering for the dinner break. Luckily, the census of the CCU has once again remained low for the past several weeks. Outside of the big TV star there is one other patient who just had a heart attack. When Jane sees me she waves me over to the medication room.

"Great timing Steele," she says as she puts a morphine cartridge in the syringe. "Watch me waste five milligrams so I can give this guy his nighttime dose."

I watch as she pushes half of the morphine out of the syringe into the sink. This little maneuver is supposed to keep us on the up and up. I sign the narcotics log stating that I witnessed the wasting of the unnecessary morphine. Jane goes to give the morphine to the patient while I continue my rounds.

I get bored and page Storm.

"Just wanted to let you know I love you," I say.

"Same here babe," he says back. "I am on my way up to the unit for my last rounds. How about we neck in your office?"

Ah, the privileges of leadership.

Storm knocks on my office door just as his beeper goes off again. He glances at the read out.

"Stat page CCU."

I am immediately annoyed. Not only are these patients inconsiderate of my love life but they are beginning to piss me off. I decide to implement new rules. No more acute illness on the evening shift. All cardiac arrests and heart attacks will take place on the day and night shifts from now on. I already have the memo drafted in my head as I run with Storm to the CCU.

Jane is standing there with the fresh heart attack patient giving him oxygen. He is pale and doing his best impression of getting ready to meet Jesus.

"I just don't understand it," Jane says nervously. "I just gave him his regularly scheduled dose of morphine about fifteen minutes ago. Everything was fine. Then he started to sour."

I take the med keys from Jane and go for more morphine. When I come back I slip the needle into the IV tubing and give him another five milligrams. The patient responds within seconds. Storm and I exchange a look. Something is not right here. When Jane gives patients morphine they still have chest pain. When I give them the morphine their chest pain goes away.

After the patient is stable Storm and I leave the CCU and head back to my office. Both of us are silent.

When we get to my office we step inside and look at each other.

"Something funny is going on in the CCU babe," Storm says.

"As sure as shit."

"So what do we do?"

I pause before I say, "Ask the big-time TV star?"

"Sounds about right to me."

Jane has the next night off. I keep a close eye on the CCU. Everything seems fine. The big-time TV star seems down. I try to think of all sorts of wonderful nursing interventions and uplifting things to say. Naturally, I fail.

"So what's up your ass tonight?" I say to the big-time TV star.

"Not you faggot boy!"

She wipes her runny nose on her sleeve. Ah, the elegance of Hollywood.

"So, you are missing your little drug buddy tonight? Must be hard when your in-house supplier is away."

Big TV star's eyes widen to saucers.

"I think you girls have been sharing some of the goodies," I say as I cross my arms and stare directly at her. "That is why you came down to the on-call room. You were suppose to meet Jane there, but we had that little nasty nosebleed incident instead."

After a long silence she says, "You know, you sure are smart for a queer boy."

I smile. "You are going to help me catch Jane in the act."

"Fuck off!"

I bend over to her and calmly say, "It is simple really. Either you help or I call up the editor of *The New York Times* and tell him that you are a cokehead stealing drugs from the hospital and placing patients' lives in jeopardy. I think that number-one rated sitcom of yours would be history before I could put the phone down."

Storm has walked up behind me. He puts his hands on my shoulders and gives me a squeeze. "Just think of it as another acting job, but with a limited audience."

The big-time TV star plops down into a chair drained.

I cannot believe that Jane is stealing morphine from patients. I am furious. When patients have chest pain and need morphine it is to save their lives, not only to make them feel better. Jane could literally kill somebody by not giving them their morphine.

The three of us plot the setup for the next night. I figure it is time to call on my old buddy Daisy McQueen again and let her know what is going on. I call Daisy from my office and explain to her that I believe Jane is stealing morphine and why. I also tell her of the big-time TV star's confession that she is getting drugs from Jane.

Daisy is stonily silent on the other end.

"You there?" I finally say.

"You sure about this?"

"Totally."

"Okay, I will come in tomorrow night and fire the bitch. Call me in my office when you catch her."

We hang up.

The plan is very simple. We just let Jane do her usual thing in the CCU the following night and have the big-time TV star set a time to meet her for the sale of the morphine. Just for sentiment's sake we use the now-famous on-call room as the place where the deal goes down. Also, I figure Storm and I can hide in the bathroom. Who knows, maybe we could have some tearoom sex while we wait. Nurses are very productive. We never let a moment go by when there is something to do.

It goes as planned and I make sure that the patients get their morphine after Jane slips them salt water instead of the real drug.

The big-time TV star asks Jane for help getting high and agrees to meet her in the on-call room at 11 p.m. I let Daisy McQueen know what is going on.

Storm and I get to the on-call room just before eleven to make sure everything is okay. I curse myself for being so punctual. I look at my watch and realize we won't have time for sex. We open the bathroom door and Daisy McQueen flashes into focus when we turn on the light. She is dressed in a red jumper with a smashing orange and green polka-dot blouse with sleeves that billow out like a matador's. She fills the tiny bathroom with her size and costume.

"Holy fuck Daisy!" I nearly scream. "You nearly gave me a heart attack. What the hell are you doing here?"

"That getup is about to give me one!" Storm says as he clutches his hand to his chest.

"You like it?" she says as she twirls around for a full view.

"Fabulous, if you are into clown sex." I pause. "Are you sure you are lesbian?" I say eyeing her more closely.

"Doesn't my fashion sense make that pretty clear?"

"Thank God lesbians don't do drag."

"You don't think this isn't drag?!"

Before we can exchange any more intellectual points on lesbian fashion I hear noise outside of the on-call room door. Great, Jane and the big-time TV star are on time also.

"Quick! Get in." I jump up on the toilet seat to make room for Storm and Daisy. However, the old physics principle of two pieces of matter not being able to occupy the same space at the same time has not vanished. Daisy is knocked into the shower stall while Storm consumes the tiny space in front of the sink. Behind the glass door of the shower stall Daisy looks like Bozo in a bottle. This is the side of detective work they tactfully leave off on television.

We can hear Jane and the big-time TV star talking but not exactly what they are saying. I realize we forgot to set up some sort of signal for the big-time TV star to alert us when to pounce. I am about to whisper my concern to Storm when he suddenly ducks as Daisy McQueen goes flying over his head. She looks like an angry rainbow about to vomit.

She kicks out the bathroom door and blasts into the on-call room.

"Freeze fucker!" she screams. Storm and I stumble out behind her.

Jane and the big-time TV star are in the middle of the drug trade. Daisy is braced in a martial arts stance that I am sure would be considered immoral in most Southern states.

Jane's mouth drops open and the big-time TV star pretends to faint.

"God, that was orgasmic!" Daisy says. I think I almost see her smile.

Jane is fired and arrested. Two events that I am surprised I have not yet experienced. Storm tells me to be patient and that my time will come.

The big-time TV star is discharged and is forced to buy her drugs on the street like everyone else.

I am promoted to evening head nurse. Storm and I decide to live together. Life is very interesting.

I call to tell my mother of our decision to live together. She is beside herself.

"You mean to tell me you are going to live together without the benefit of marriage?!"

"Ma, gay people are not allowed to get married," I point out.

"Who says?" she wants to know.

"The church, the government, society in general."

"Bullshit!"

"It's the truth."

"Well, double bat shit to that! You are going to have a nice ceremony and reception. I will see to it. You don't worry about anything. I will take care of this."

I am sure she will.

"Boy, am I going to blast a nasty letter off to the Pope," she says.

I make the sign of the Cross as I hang up.

Storm is on call and I am restless. I call Harry. I want to go out for drink at Auntie Em's for old time's sake. I have not been there in months since I started dating Storm.

"Cheating on your boyfriend before you even move in with him?" Harry asks.

"Don't be an idiot," I reply. "I actually miss you. I haven't seen you or Carmella in ages. Thought it would be nice to catch up."

"And here I thought that you wanted to be a trashy slut."

"My trashy slut days are over."

"So now I have to carry the entire burden. Thanks."

"Harry, I have seen you carry an entire troop of Boy Scouts."

"You know a real friend would not mention ugly memories."

"Go figure."

I arrive at Auntie Em's around seven. Carmella and Harry are already there. I live a ten-minute walk away and they beat me to the bar.

"How in the hell did you guys get here so soon?"

Carmella beams up. "That hot little pink car can sure tear ass!"

"You borrowed my mother's car?"

"Nope," says Harry. "She drove."

"My mother is here! In a gay bar!"

"Well, *I* am in a gay bar," says Carmella.

"But you are a fag hag," I gently remind her.

"So I want to become one too," my mother says as she emerges from the crowd in the other room.

She is dressed in a day-glow orange Nehru suit with enough love beads to jump rope. She looks like a priest just ordained by Sammy Davis Jr. I briefly think about introducing her to Daisy McQueen. However, I remind myself I am a nurse. The sight of my mother and Daisy in whatever outfits together would probably cause mass hysteria. I make a mental note to pick out her clothes for the commitment ceremony.

"Let's have a drink," my mother says as she taps the side her fake-fruit-laden straw bag. I suspect she has just mugged a drag queen doing Carmen Miranda.

"Ma, you don't drink."

"I do *now*. Hell, I am old. What am I waiting for?" she says as she steps up to the bar. "Give me a boilermaker!" She slaps her hand on the bar for effect. "Hey, what the hell? Make it a double!"

"For crap's sake, Ma. That will kill you." I look at Bernie and stare him down. "My mother will have a glass of white wine."

"On the rocks," she adds. "And don't you dare put in any of those sissy umbrellas. I want a *real* drink."

"One real white wine on the rocks sans umbrella coming right up," Bernie says with kindness and boredom.

Great, I think, I am now going to have to teach my mother how to drink.

Carmella has tactfully secured four bar stools for us by lying across them like a corpse. Her eyes are closed and her hands folded in repose across her chest. Very realistic except for the fact she has a cigarette in her mouth and is blowing the smoke out her nose. I decide to quit smoking on the spot.

I make this announcement as Carmella rises from the dead and we all take our seats.

"If my mother can start drinking I can stop smoking." I reason as Bernie takes the rest of our drink order. "After all, my boyfriend is a cardiac surgeon and I cannot be smoking around him."

Harry raises an eyebrow. "Just like that?"

"Yup, just like that."

"Wow," my mother says as she gulps down half of her white wine. "That Storm must be some hot number in bed for you to give up cigarettes."

"This is where I draw the line. I will not discuss my sex life with my mother."

"Why not?" says Bernie. "She has been discussing *your* sex life with everyone before you got here." He places the drinks down in front of us.

I glare at my mother. "What have you been doing?"

"Just a little research," she says as she downs the last of her wine. Bernie brings her another one before I can protest. "I understand that being good in the sack is very important in the homosexual community. So I asked around a little."

Carmella sticks her finger in her drink and stirs it. "So how did he do?"

My mother turns to her and says, "He must be some hot pants! He got rated a 9.2. Just look." My mother points to the far end of the bar. Three vaguely familiar men are holding up cocktail napkins with scores on them just like at the Olympics. I take a big slug of my drink and pretend I am not in a gay bar with my mother, my best friends, and forgotten tricks that have rated my sexual performance to my mother. Once again, I fail.

I signal Bernie for a refill and tell him to cut my mother off. He leans into me and whispers that he has been giving her ginger ale. I notice a funny mark on his face. It sort of looks like a nasty bruise under his left eye.

"Hey Bernie," I say pointing to the purple spot. "What happened?"

"Damned if I know. Just showed up a few days ago."

Harry looks at Bernie's bruise. "You've been jumping rope naked again?"
I do not like the look of it. I plan to bring Storm by and have him give
Bernie the once-over.

The rest of the evening is fairly uneventful. My mother slugged down
three ginger ales thinking they were wine, got tipsy by placebo effect, and
drove off in the night in her big pink car with Harry and Carmella soundly
asleep in the back seat.

As I get back to my apartment the phone rings.

It is my mother. "I want you to get me Storm's father's phone number."

"Why?" I ask slowly.

"Didn't you tell me he was a retired priest?"

"Yes. An Episcopal priest."

"Perfect! The damn Episcopalians will do *anything*. Hell, they even have
women priests!" she laughs into the end of her receiver.

"Sorry, must be the white wine," she says calming herself.

"Must be," I say. "So why do you want his phone number?"
I brace myself for the obvious reply.

"So he can perform the ceremony."

Now, why didn't I think of *that*.

My mother is taking this planning out our ceremony too seriously. She is
driving me crazy. I try to be mad at her but I can't. Storm thinks it is wonderful. He cannot wait for me to meet his father. Suddenly my life has become a twisted and prolonged episode of *Ozzie and Harriet*.

After this whirlwind romance and ICU antics I realize that I never did
make it to Storm's apartment. Where are we going to live? Surely not in my
tiny apartment. When I tell Storm my concerns he just smiles and says,
"You'll see."

Storm and I are standing in the living room of his apartment on Gay
Street in Greenwich Village. It is enormous and incredibly beautiful. It is
two floors of brownstone in the middle of the block. By quick count there
are eight rooms, including a formal dining room with a fireplace, three bed-
rooms, and a library. There is even a garage.

I am stunned. "How in the world do you afford the rent on this palace on a resident's salary?"

"I own it babe. I don't rent. I own the whole building including the top apartment." Storm pauses then looks at me. "Did I forget to tell you I am rich?"

"Rich? How rich?" My eyes are about to dance outside my head.

"Filthy. When my mother was killed my dad got a very large insurance settlement. He invested it extremely wisely and before you know it we were millionaires."

"You forgot to mention this because . . . ?"

"I did not want to scare you away. Most guys I have dated got weird about it, and I fell in love with you that night I saw you in the ICU. I didn't want to chance anything going wrong."

My heart melts.

"I figure that we can move your mother in on the top floor someday."

"You are saying that just to drive me nuts."

"Babe," he says as he takes me in his arms. "For you it is only a short walk."

"What about your father?"

"Room for him next door."

"You own the building next door?"

"Actually, this whole side of the block."

I try not to be impressed with Storm's money. I fail. Then I remember that Storm is not impressed with his money. He could have had a life of leisure but instead he became a physician. God, I love him.

I am looking forward to going back to the unit. All this commitment ceremony planning is taking its toll on me. Getting back to the land of equal-opportunity illness has its bizarre appeal. I remind myself that psychotherapy may be in my future if this keeps up.

I am once again in the coronary care unit. Every time I enter the unit I shudder at the thoughts of Jane and the big-time TV star. Tonight there is a new admit who is sleeping peacefully. She is a ninety-two-year-old woman named Rose Garfield. She has just had her first heart attack. She is stable.

I am making rounds and acting like I know what I am doing as a manager. No one ever teaches you any principles of management in nursing school. You get promoted because you are a good clinical nurse. How in the hell that translates into being able to manage a large staff beats the hell out of me. But most things beat the hell out of me so I figure it will work out.

When I stick my head into Mrs. Garfield's cubicle she stirs. I walk in to see if she needs anything. I glance up at her monitors and they inform me everything is fine.

"May I have some water?" Mrs. Garfield says.

"Of course," I say as I pour some water into a cup and insert a straw. She drinks. She smiles. I wipe her chin with a tissue.

"You know this is the first time in fifty-two years that I have not slept in the same bed with my husband," she says as her mouth turns up in a slight smile as she shrugs her shoulders. "You know, this isn't *so* bad." She turns over and goes back to sleep.

I smile as I pat her on the arm and make sure the covers are up around her before I leave.

I am feeling benevolent about the elderly as I step into my apartment. My mother is asleep on the sofa with a half-empty bottle of beer at her side. I quickly make plans to put out a contract on the doorman. At this rate, locking my front door just seems like a huge waste of time.

I approach my mother and she smiles. I lean down and kiss her.

"May I ask what you are doing here?" I ask as I take a gander at her latest fashion choice. Jeans, high heels, and a bright yellow turtleneck sweater. All in all, not bad really, except that the heels are lavender suede stilettos and she has a cowboy hat on her head.

"Storm picked me up."

I look around the apartment and he is nowhere to be seen.

"So where is he?"

"Don't know," my mother says as she uprights herself and takes a slug of beer. "He told me to wait right here and he would be back shortly." She yarns. "How about another cold one for your old mother?"

I do not even think of voicing any concern. I want a Scotch right now and I hate to drink alone. Might as well drink with my mother. I am certain Donna Reed occasionally knocks back a few with her brood.

I go to the kitchen and fix our drinks. When I come back into the living room my mother has propped her stilettos on top of my coffee table. Circus clowns walk on shorter stilts.

"Nice shoes, " I say as I sip my drink.

"Bernie the bartender gave them to me."

Why, of course he did.

"I didn't notice him giving you anything the night we were at Auntie Em's."

"Of course not. He gave me these last night." She clicks her heals together three times. "They sure are cool!"

"Cool, " I repeat as I hear the front door open. I no longer even consider my privacy a basic human right.

In walks Storm with an older man that I have to assume is his father. This is great. My mother is dressed like a hooker and we are drinking as I am about to meet a priest and my future father-in-law. My mother recognizes the panic in my face and says, "Relax. He is an *Episcopal* priest. Retired even." She pats my arm as I jump up.

"Hey there babe," Storm says as he kisses me then my mother. "This is my daddy."

I try to sum up all the adult fibers in my body.

"It is nice to meet you Mr. Storm. I mean Father Storm. I mean Reverend Storm. Oh hell, I don't know what I mean!"

Storm's father sticks out his hand and says, "Be easier if you just call me Hale."

"Hale Storm!" my mother howls as she slugs back her beer.

"And this is my mother, Bette Steele." I do not even try to cover up for her behavior.

"That's okay little lady," says Hale smiling broadly. "My father was named Wynd."

Wynd, Hale, and Gale Storm. Am I in love with a man or a tropical depression?

Well, at least I am not naked this time. I make a mental note to never let Storm's father see my penis. The only man of the cloth that ever saw it was a crazed Lutheran seminary student I defrocked on a dare from Carmella. I suddenly realize that I am going to hell.

"My father just flew in from Texas but I wanted us all to have a chance to meet and talk about the wedding."

"Great," I say and realize I mean it. "Drinks?"

"Is the Archbishop of Canterbury light in his loafers?" Hale says and roars.

Great, now I am going to have to understand Anglican humor.

"I am sticking with my brewski," my mother announces as she pats her beer bottle.

"Scotch?"

"You sit babe," Storm says as he takes my glass. "You have been working all evening. I'll make drinks."

For the next two hours we sit and drink and talk and talk and talk. My mother has some definite ideas on the ceremony. I nix any presence of pink flamingos that my mother thinks will be just grand and gay. And no, accordion music will not be played. Nor will there be any dancing of the "Alley Cat."

"You are just an old fart," my mother informs me.

"Seems that way," Hale says. "But I understand he has a nice penis."

"It was rated a 9.2 at Auntie Em's," my mother proudly announces.

"I give it a ten," Storm beams.

As my penis becomes the topic of discussion once again the doorbell rings. I glance at my watch. It is 2 a.m. Since no one I know appears to know how to use a doorbell I assume it is a traveling salesman, a murderer, or a Jehovah's Witness with insomnia. I get up and answer the door.

No such luck. It is Harry and Carmella.

"We were just passing by and thought we would stop in," Carmella says.

"How does one pass by at two o'clock in the morning?" I inquire.

"Gently," replies Harry quietly.

"So who is up for pizza?" Carmella asks. All hands go up. One of the nice things about living in Manhattan is that it is literally open twenty-four hours a day, and everyone delivers. You can get anything from food to sex delivered to your door if you have the cash.

"I want anchovies!"

"Make sure there are meatballs!'

"Sausage too," Storm says.

Carmella calls in the order as I calculate the coronary risk of eating such an animal.

After the pizza arrives the six of us sprawl out in my tiny apartment. There are too many conversations going on for me to keep up with. I also realize it doesn't much matter since I suspect that my opinion would not carry much weight.

Through the haze of the late hour, the coronary-killing pizza, and the booze I make out snippets of conversation. I am nodding off.

"There just have to be drag queens *somewhere* that can do what we what."

"Why of course there are."

"I think a full gospel choir is almost a must."

"A brass band is always fun."

"You know, you cannot go wrong with penguins."

Around 4 a.m. I announce it is time for bed. I pull out the sofa and make it up for my mother and Storm's father to sleep on. Harry and Carmella camp out on the floor with some blankets. Storm and I go into my once-thought-to-be luxurious sleeping alcove and go to bed. I glance at the strange tableau and realize I am a lucky man. Unusual but lucky.

When I wake up, my mother, Hale, Harry, and Carmella are sitting around the table drinking coffee. I look down to see Storm's face. God, he is handsome. He is still asleep. I smile and gently kiss him on the lips.

"Then it is all settled," I overhear my mother say. "Except for the date."

"Why not next Saturday?" Harry says.

"Why not," my mother responds

Why not indeed. I just close my eyes and snuggle under Storm's arm. We are going to be married next Saturday, somewhere in Manhattan with a drag queen doing God knows what, some form of music that will make my skin crawl, and, of course, the always-popular penguins.

When I wake up again Storm and I are alone and we take advantage of it and make love.

Storm and I decide that our honeymoon will have to wait until he gets done with his residency. It is going to be hard enough getting a long week-end off for the ceremony. Then I remember I am now the boss and give myself a four-day weekend. Storm already has arranged coverage with another doc so we are all set to go. Expect now panic sets in. How in the hell are we going to do everything in a week's time?

"Babe, this is where being rich is actually fun. Your mother is taking care of calling everyone. My father has booked a banquet room at Tavern on the Green. I have arranged for several suites at the Plaza. All you have to do is get fitted for you tuxedo and show up."

With astonishing speed everything falls into place. Storm waves his magic wand over everything and it all just falls into place. My apartment is packed up and moved to our new home on Gay Street. I am picked up in a car and driven to Barneys and fitted for the world's most beautiful tuxedo. My mother is whisked away to Lord and Taylor's armed with a personal shopper. Harry and Carmella plan my bachelor party.

I have so little to do with anything I think about getting a dog just to fill my time.

"The bachelor party is all set," Carmella informs me over the phone. "This Thursday night at Auntie Em's."

"I didn't know gay men had bachelor parties."

"Well pudding lips," she replies. "I didn't know gay men got married."

"Actually, I have *no* idea what the hell is going on."

"Why should you? Don't you trust us?"

"Would you trust you?"

"Good point."

Carmella hangs up.

Gay marriages, like gay bachelor parties, are an evolving social custom. There are no set rules. However, it is the mid-1980s and I figure that a new decade should bring in new ideas.

Everyone is invited. Storm, myself, my mother, Hale, Carmella, Harry, and everyone from the ICU. The only person missing is Myles. I am relieved. I guess my little birthday cake incident has firmly put him at a distance.

Auntie Em's is closed to the general public for the party. We arrive at 7 p.m. and the place is packed with everyone we know. There is a ten-foot-high cake in the middle of the room. I can only assume that some male stripper is going to pop out of it. I resign myself to the inevitable.

My mother is knocking back some frothy concoction with Daisy McQueen at the far end of the bar. My mother is dressed all in leather with a yellow-and-green-striped halter top. She has on boots anyone in the Third Reich would have killed for. Daisy is in a paisley muumuu that could hide a car full of clowns. Together they represent an awesome force of nature.

Bernie is behind the bar naked except for a leather jockstrap. Carmella and Harry are hosting a bizarre drinking game of sorts in the next room. Music is playing. People are happy and I am with the man I love.

I take Storm over to meet Bernie and get a drink. I suddenly remember the bruise and whisper to Storm to take a look at it. He nods.

"Bernie, this is Storm, the man I am to marry even though it is against the law and the church."

"Nice to meet you," Bernie says as he sticks out his hand for Storm to shake.

"Great jockstrap by the way."

Bernie snaps the waistband and grins. "Steele's mother is one hell of a shopper. She made me try on every leather jockstrap at this store on Christopher Street before we could settle on this number." He thrusts his ample crotch forward and laughs.

Bernie hands us our drinks and we walk bravely into the crowd.

"So what do you think of that bruise on Bernie's face?" I ask Storm.

"Don't know babe, but I don't like it. You know there is that report out about some new cancer that was seen in gay men in California. Don't know much about it but I guess we should start looking into it." Storm pauses. "Look, after the wedding we will come back and have another look at it. But tonight it is about us. Agreed?"

"Yes doctor," I smirk.

He pats my ass and laughs.

People are milling about and seem to be having a pretty good time. Gloria is dancing with Mary Butler. Judi, Jill, and Mrs. Day are staring at the cake. As I look around the room I realize I actually don't know about half the people in the bar. Oh, well. Some days chicken, some days feathers. I am sure I will know them by the end of the party.

"Storm, what the hell are we supposed to do here?"

"In the South when a man is in a bar he usually drinks."

"Good," I say. I can handle this. "Time for a refill?"

"You bet babe."

I hear laughter come from all sections of the bar. Bernie refills our drinks and as I head back over to Storm the door to the bar bursts open. In walks a cowboy. I look harder. I cannot believe this. It is not just any cowboy, it is a Sky King impersonator! I nearly drop my jaw and look for my mother. She is laughing so hard that she nearly tips over her bar stool.

"I have been waiting to do this to you since you were in grade school!"

Sky King walks in and jumps up on the bar. Everyone is looking. Storm comes up behind me. Sky King motions me over with his finger. I freeze. This has been my fantasy since I was a little boy. Storm gently nudges me toward Sky King.

Sky King gets down on his knees and kisses me on the cheek.

"This is from your mother."

With that said he bounces back up to a standing position, signals the disc jockey, and suddenly the room is filled with disco music. Sky King grinds his hips and rips off his shirt. He is phenomenal. Every muscle of his torso is like etched glass.

Someone is loudly yelling for him to take it all off. I am only mildly surprised to realize that it is my mother.

He struts up and down the bar like a pro and wiggles his butt to the point where I think Bernie is going to commit a mortal sin. He slowly opens his jeans and plays with his crotch. I am sure this is what married life is going to be like every night.

Daisy McQueen has jumped up on the pool table and is gyrating to the music in her muumuu with a pool stick flung across her shoulders.

Sky King rips his jeans off and is naked expect for his cowboy hat and a scant jockstrap.

"Yippee!" my mother yells pounding on the bar. "Show us the good stuff!"

Mrs. Day pulls out a rosary and begins to pray.

With that Sky King grinds his hips and rips off the jockstrap. I am awestruck. I did not think it genetically possible for a white man's penis to be that big. I resist the urge to salute.

The crowd cheers and Sky King tosses his hat into the air. Daisy catches it and is now doing some sort of a Mexican hat dance. Meanwhile, Sky King stands naked on the bar with his hands on his hips.

Judi runs up to him, her hair following from behind and says, "I just have to touch it honey. I have seen fire hoses smaller than your dick." Judi gently squeezes it. Sky King just grins and grins and grins.

"Dear lesbian lord above. This fucker is real!" Judi places a hand to her mouth and steps back in amazement.

Bernie hands Sky King a bathrobe before the rest of the bar starts yanking at his chain. Storm and I are laughing too hard to notice that the music has changed, and that the cake in the middle of the room is being turned around by Bernie. A rousing rendition of "Everything's Coming Up Roses" is heating up the dance floor as Linda Harper vaults out of the top of the cake singing at the top of her lungs. Everyone is stunned. Even my mother.

I turn toward Storm. "Did you have anything to do with this?"

"Nope, I tried to get the big-time TV star but I was told she was in rehab in Westchester." Well, so much for peace in suburbia.

I catch Gloria and Mary Butler laughing in our direction. Of course it had to be them.

Linda Harper is guided down the cake by Bernie on one side and Sky King on the other. She comes over and kisses me. She just looks at Storm.

"And you must be the husband-to-be," Linda says. "Guess I was not good enough to convert you full time," she says to me.

"You slept with Linda Harper and forgot to tell me?" Storm's eyes arc in amazement.

"Oh honey we did NOT sleep. We fucked for hours. You are one lucky man. He is a great fuck and he has such a nice penis."

"It was rated a 9.2," my mother yells through cupped hands.

"As nice as this," Sky King asks as he opens his bathrobe.

"Ohmygod!" Linda says as she backs away astonished. "Does it have it's own name?"

"I call him Charlie!" beams Sky King.

Linda Harper looks at me. "Well I think Charlie has got you beat by at least a mile." She pauses. "I think I mean that literally."

"Oh well. Some days chicken, some days feathers," I say as I spread open my hands.

"Oh honey, forget about chicken! Tonight it is all about pork!" Linda Harper laughs as she pulls Sky King to the door by his penis.

"Holy Christ Lady! I'm gay!" he protests.

"That is what they all say. My limo is out here and we are going to play!"

"Be gentle with him," I call after them.

"Mind your own damn business," yells back Sky King as they head out the door.

The noise in the bar returns to normal like nothing has happened. You just cannot phase an ICU nurse.

"Can someone tell me just what the hell happened here?" I say to no one in particular.

"Your mother hired a stripper who looks like Sky King, your first boy-hood crush. He stripped, and showed us his penis. Which was considerable. Linda Harper, whom you have fucked, it appears, jumped out of a cake and sang a song, and by my impression is now saddling up Sky King's pony somewhere on Third Avenue in her limo," Carmella says.

"That seems like an accurate statement of events," Harry agrees.

The evening drifts into a succession of blurry events and I magically find myself tucked into bed at our suite at the Plaza. I turn over and Storm is there.

"I love you," I say.

"Love you too, " he says as he presses into me. "Everyone is safely back at the hotel and I asked security to keep an eye on your mother. I can only *imagine* what your mother would do if left to her own devices at the Plaza in the middle of the night."

"No, you can't actually."

"You are right. I can't."

"But I can."

I shudder slightly as we fall asleep in each other's arms.

I awake in the morning realizing that I am about to be married. Excitement and fear grip me. I am a very lucky man. My life has fallen into a happiness pie.

The ceremony at Tavern on the Green will be simple, elegant, and tasteful I am told. No drag queens, obnoxious music or penguins will appear anywhere. The room is decorated with huge bouquets of white tulips. Magnums of champagne stand guard in buckets of ice. Soft piano music fills the air.

People are milling about talking quietly before the ceremony begins. My mother arrives, thanks to Lord and Taylor and Storm's bank book, in a soft pink chiffon dress. She looks beautiful. She is truly happy and so am I. As I stare at my mother I hear noise coming from the entrance to the hall.

"Of course I'm fucking invited!"

Then I hear words that I cannot make out.

"No, I do NOT have my invitation. It was stolen along with everything else." The voice goes up a notch and I recognize it at once. "I am Daisy *fucking* McQueen!"

That being said enter one Daisy *fucking* McQueen. She is dressed in a chocolate Chanel suit with low black pumps and a matching handbag. I immediately wonder what alien has invaded her body. She is stunning. She catches me staring at her and comes marching over.

"Don't get me started Steele. This is the only thing I had to wear. Got up this morning to find a note saying all my clothes had been taken hostage until tomorrow. All they left was this damn get up." She moves her hands disgustingly around her body. "Probably some damn dyke idea of a joke. Lesbian humor is lost on me. You think I want to look like this?" She shudders.

Before I can respond she stomps away.

"You stole her clothes?" I ask Storm.

"I am a gentleman," he responds.

"But I'm not," says Carmella coming up from behind.

"How in the world?"

"Simple really. I just dropped five mgs of Valium in her last drink last night and saw her home. She went down like a nun on a gun."

"You slipped a mickey to one of the directors of nursing?" My eyebrows arch to the ceiling.

"Oh please, like it doesn't happen all the time."

Why of course it does, I say to myself.

I scan the room and all the usual suspects are in place. I feel a gentle tap on my shoulder. It is my mother. Her eyes are misting.

"Mom, don't." I foolishly begin to protest. I begin to cry also.

"Why not?" she says dabbing her eyes. "Today my only child is getting married. A mother is supposed to cry."

"You're right. Why not?" I say gently and bend down and kiss her. Hale comes up to us.

"What do you say we go and break some religious and civil laws and get our children married?"

Hale gathers us into the center of the room and everyone stands around us in semicircle. Harry, Carmella, and my mother are the closest to me, and I realize, that is the way it is supposed to be.

Hale is reciting words from *The Book of Common Prayer* and I am trying to pay attention. However, all I can do is think how incredibly happy I am. How lucky I am. Everything sounds muffled to me. I wonder if Storm is hearing any of his father's words. People are gently crying the happy tears of commitment. Daisy McQueen opens her purse and pulls out a red and purple polka-dot handkerchief and blows her nose. I smile, it seems Carmella forgot to rifle through her dresser drawers.

My mother nudges me in my side to respond with the traditional "I do." I can barely speak and Storm just smiles at me. Rings get slipped on our fingers and I am still having an out-of-body experience. As we kiss, the room breaks into cheers and music fills the air. Everyone is hugging everyone.

Waiters enter the room with trays of champagne. Joy is in the air.

Storm and I are walking through the crowd greeting people. Snippets of conversations fly around us.

Tea sandwiches are being circulated on large silver platters. A glass is being clinked by silverware. Storm and I turn around. Hale and my mother are standing at the head table with their glasses raised. Everyone quiets down.

My mother speaks first. "We are two very happy and proud parents here today. Our boys have just given us great happiness." Tears well up in her voice. Storm squeezes my hand.

"Bette and I feel blessed," Hale says. "We each love our sons and are happy they have found each other. We wish them a lifetime of love and happiness."

Everyone raises their glasses and the toast is official. My mother downs her champagne like a pro.

"And it ain't so bad that my son-in-law is stinking rich!" my mother says. "This old lady is really gonna live!"

"Hell, me too!" Hale shouts.

Everyone laughs.

Carmella comes up to me. "I cannot believe you are married."

"Neither can I."

"I suppose this means that our bar-hopping days are over."

"I shouldn't think so. The only thing different is I won't be cruising for sex."

Harry slides up to us. "You never cruised. You begged."

"Okay, so there were some ugly times."

"Honey, there were times when I wanted to throw you a pity telethon."

"Got that right." Carmella says as she sticks another cigarette in her mouth. She is wearing a hat with a veil that blows upward with every stream of smoke.

"Well, if my memory serves me correctly neither one of you have had a *date* in years."

"We are in a cult," Carmella says. "We are only allowed meaningless screws."

"Speaking of which," Harry groans. "I think it is time to shake my booty at that nice Irish waiter over at the bar. I want to kiss his Blarney Stone tonight."

The rest of the weekend passes in a blur of laughter, lovemaking, and champagne. My mother and Hale share one suite and Harry and Carmella another. Actually the only time we get alone is when we go to bed.

On Sunday night Storm says, "I am sorry we cannot go on a honeymoon now. But as soon as my residency is over we'll go whereever you want."

"Where would you like to go?"

"It really doesn't matter as long as we are together."

I smile and grab his hand.

"God, I love you."

"I love you too babe."

Storm and I both have late starts at the hospital on Monday. When I get to my office the staff has papered hearts and wedding bells all over the place. I can barely move around without hitting one of them. I smile some warm thoughts and wonder how many fire codes have been violated on my account.

I hear a voice shout.

"I have a code situation here!" It is coming from the medical ICU.

I run, ripping through all the decorations. Paper wedding bells die by the dozens as I trample my way to the code.

I make my way into the MICU and see the code in progress. Gloria is still there from the day shift and is doing chest compressions. A respiratory therapist is bagging oxygen into the patient while the rest of the staff insert IVs and gives meds.

Gloria spies me and says, "Steele, maybe you should sit this one out."

I am confused. Then I see what she means.

The patient being coded is Bernie the bartender.

I look at him, "What the hell happened?"

Gloria continues to pump Bernie's chest, "He was admitted on Sunday. They think it is some sort of strange pneumonia. Maybe related to GRID or AIDS. Whatever the hell they are calling it this week." Gloria pauses. "He was fine on rounds a few minutes ago. Can someone take over for me please?"

Another nurse kneels on the bed and continues chest compressions as Gloria comes my way. "I'm so sorry Steele. I was just about to come to your office and let you know that Bernie was admitted when he soured. They can handle this without us." Gloria gently leads me out of the unit and back to my office.

I rip all the goddamn decorations down and cry. I begin to have shaking sobs and Gloria holds me in her arms. After a few minutes I stop and look at her.

"You know, Gloria, I have been so caught up with my own life, I just let a lot of things slip by. I have been hearing all the reports of gay cancer but I didn't pay them any attention. I even noticed what I thought was a bruise on Bernie's face and it didn't register. I am a jerk."

"No, you're just human."

"Storm and I were going to go back to Auntie Em's this week and take a look at that damn lesion again. Now this." I begin to cry again.

Words are not spoken and sometimes this is best. Gloria and I sit in silence. I make a silent vow to become an expert on this new disease.

Minutes stretch by endlessly. There is a soft knock at my office door and Storm enters. His face is gray.

"They just called it babe. Bernie's gone."

I just look at him. "Gone?"

Gloria gently leans forward. "Bernie's dead, Steele."

Bernie's funeral is attended by hundreds of people. I have no idea who most of them are. Storm and I sit in the back of the church with my mother and Hale. Carmella and Harry are next to us.

The service begins with a woman standing in the middle of the altar. She sings "Amazing Grace" a cappella with a clear and haunting voice, and I feel my throat tighten. A tear falls down Storm's cheek. My mother is grim-faced. And everyone else is just numb.

After a moment of silence the singer speaks, "I am Mary Lawrence. I am Bernie's sister. I would like to thank you all for coming. I am overwhelmed by the number of people that were touched by Bernie's life. Bernie and I became very close over the past few years. I was the first person he told about having this new 'gay cancer'." She pauses. She chokes up.

"It's funny, really. Somehow I just didn't really take it seriously. The information that is out there is hard to understand and there isn't much of it. I assumed that it would eventually just go away. I mean, what disease attacks because someone is gay? Now, we are beginning to know." My mother squeezes my knee.

I sit through the rest of the funeral and feel overwhelmed. All I want to do is run out of the church and find out everything I can about this gay disease. I curse myself for being so out of it. Maybe if I had been paying more attention none of this would have happened.

The funeral ends and we leave the church.

"I think we just witnessed the beginning of something horrible," says Carmella.

"I think you are right," I say as I shudder.

"I, for one," my mother announces, "am mad as all holy hell!" She takes a tissue out of her bag and blows her nose.

"It is time for us to fight. I do not know what is going on but I will and then I am going to fight this damn disease. Let some other little old lady run the fucking Christmas fairs."

I smile at my mother. Now I know where I get my "save-the-world" complex from.

Storm and I are exhausted when we get back to our house. Dealing with death is never easy and we try to talk about it but are just too spent. We go to bed and hold each other tightly as we fall asleep.

Somewhere in the middle of the night I stumble out of bed to go to the bathroom. I splash some cool water on my face and that is when I see it. Right by my left ear is a small, irregular-shaped purple lesion. I stare at it for a long time. I try to rub it off. I start to feel sick to my stomach.

I hear Storm say from the doorway, "You okay babe?"

I slowly turn toward him and point to the lesion.

It takes him a moment to register the fact that I have the same kind of lesion that Bernie had.

"Babe," he stammers. "I am sure it is nothing. Just a bruise."

"Bullshit," I say as tears come to my eyes. He takes me in his arms and holds me.

"I'm scared."

"Me too."

I look up at him and see fear and love in his face. He holds me to his chest.

"Some days chicken, some days feathers," I say softly.

ABOUT THE AUTHOR

Richard S. Ferri, much to everyone's amazement, has three graduate degrees: two master's degrees and a doctorate. He has learned that no one needs three graduate degrees. He is also a nurse practitioner specializing in HIV/AIDS. People actually trust him. Dr. Ferri is often amazed by the general lack of good judgement that prevails in society. He is past national president of both the Association of Nurses in AIDS Care and the HIV/AIDS Nursing Certification Board. Both organizations cannot seem to keep him at bay. Dr. Ferri is an elected fellow of the American Academy of Nursing, and is certain that the Academy is revamping their election criteria to keep others like him from weaseling in. He lives in Provincetown, Massachusetts, and drinks martinis. He was managing editor of *NUMEDX* from 2001 to 2005. His work has appeared in the *Boston Globe, POZ, The Advocate,* and the *Lambda Literary Review* to cite a few. His short story "Shopping with Alice" won a fiction prize from *POZ* magazine. You can also hear him occasionally rant commentary on National Public Radio. When not sipping gin, you can usually find him collecting sea glass on the beach and talking to his dog. Dr. Ferri does not dance.